P9-CCY-804

PiPPi
Longstocking

For Quincy — L.C.

VIKING
Published by Penguin Group
Penguin Young Readers Group, 345 Hudson Street, New York, New York 10014, U.S.A.
Penguin Group (Canada), 90 Eglinton Avenue East, Suite 700, Toronto, Ontario, Canada
M4P 2Y3 (a division of Pearson Penguin Canada Inc.)

Penguin Books Ltd, Registered Offices: 80 Strand, London WC2R 0RL, England

First published in Sweden as *Pippi Långstrump* by Rabén & Sjögren, 1945
First published in the United States of America by The Viking Press, 1950
This newly translated and illustrated edition first published in the UK by Oxford University Press,
and in the United States of America by Viking, a division of Penguin Young Readers Group, 2007
This edition published by Viking, a division of Penguin Young Readers Group, 2011

10   9   8   7   6   5   4   3   2   1

LIBRARY OF CONGRESS CATALOGING-IN-PUBLICATION DATA
Lindgren, Astrid, 1907–2002.
[Pippi Långstrump. English]
Pippi Longstocking / by Astrid Lindgren ; translated by Tiina Nunnally ;
illustrated by Lauren Child.
p. cm.
Summary: Escapades of a lucky little girl who lives with a horse and a monkey—but without any
parents—at the edge of a Swedish village.
ISBN-13: 978-0-670-06276-8 (hardcover)
[1. Humorous stories.] I. Nunnally, Tiina, date– II. Child, Lauren, ill. III. Title.
PZ7.L6585Pi 2007
[Fic]—dc22   2007012419

This edition ISBN 978-0-670-01404-0

Manufactured in China
Set in Linotype Really

Astrid Lindgren

illustrated by
Lauren Child

Pippi
Longstocking

translated by Tiina Nunnally

VIKING

CONTENTS

Chapter One

Pippi Moves into Villa Villekulla

On the outskirts of a tiny little town was a neglected garden. In the garden stood an old house, and in that house lived Pippi Longstocking. She was nine years old, and she lived there all alone. She had no mother or father, which was actually quite nice, because it meant that no one could tell her that she had to go to bed just when she was having the most fun. And no one could make her take cod liver oil when she would rather eat candy.

Once upon a time Pippi did have a father whom she loved very much. And of course she once had a mother too, but that was so long ago that she couldn't remember her at all. Her mother died when Pippi was a tiny little baby, lying in her crib and crying so terribly that no one could stand to come near. Pippi thought that her mother was now up in heaven, peering down at her daughter through a hole.

Pippi would often wave to her and say, "Don't worry! I can always look after myself!"

But Pippi had not forgotten her father. He was a sea captain who sailed the great seas, and Pippi had sailed with him on his ship until one day a big storm blew him overboard and he disappeared. But Pippi was sure that one day he would come back. She didn't believe he had drowned. She believed he had washed ashore on an island that was inhabited by natives and her father had become king of them all. He walked around wearing a gold crown on his head all day long.

"My mamma is an angel, and my pappa is king of the natives. Not all children have such fine parents, let me tell you," Pippi used to say with delight. "And as soon as my pappa builds himself a ship, he'll come back to get me, and then I'll be a native princess. Yippee, what fun that will be!"

Many years ago her father had bought the old house that stood in the garden. He had planned to live there with Pippi when he grew old and was no longer able to sail the seas. Then, unfortunately, he was blown overboard. While Pippi was waiting for him to come back, she headed straight home to Villa Villekulla. That was what the house was called. It stood there, all furnished and ready—just waiting for her to arrive.

One beautiful summer evening she said good-bye to all the sailors on her father's ship. They were very fond of Pippi, and Pippi was very fond of them.

"Good-bye, boys," said Pippi, kissing each of them on the forehead, one after the other. "Don't worry about me. I can always look after myself!"

Two things she took from the ship. A little monkey whose name was Mr. Nilsson—he was a present from her father—and a big suitcase full of gold coins. The sailors stood at the railing with their eyes fixed on

Pippi for as long as they could see her. She walked firmly away without looking back. Mr. Nilsson sat on her shoulder, and she carried the suitcase in one hand.

"What an amazing child," said one of the sailors, and he wiped a tear from his eye as Pippi disappeared in the distance.

He was right. Pippi was quite an amazing child. The most amazing thing about her was that she was so strong. She was so incredibly strong that there wasn't a policeman in the whole wide world who was as strong as she was. She could lift a whole horse if she wanted to. And she did. She had her own horse that she had bought with one of her many gold coins on the very same day that she arrived home at Villa Villekulla. She had always longed to have her own horse. He now lived on the porch. Whenever Pippi wanted to have her afternoon coffee there, she would simply lift him down into the garden.

Next to Villa Villekulla was another garden with another house. In that house lived a father and a mother with their two sweet children, a boy and a girl. The boy's name was Tommy, and the girl's name was Annika. They were two very nice, well-mannered, and obedient children. Tommy never bit his fingernails, and he always did whatever his mother asked him to do. Annika never made a fuss if she wasn't allowed to have her own way, and she always looked so dainty in her crisply ironed little cotton dresses, which she was careful not to get dirty.

Tommy and Annika played very nicely together in their garden, but they had often wished for a playmate. While Pippi was still sailing the seas with her father, they would sometimes lean over the fence and say to each other, "It's so sad that no one has ever moved into that house! Someone should live there, someone with children."

On that beautiful summer evening when Pippi stepped through the front door of Villa Villekulla for the very first time, Tommy and Annika were not at home. They had gone to visit their grandmother for a week. That's why they had no idea that someone had moved into the house next door. On the first day after they came home, when they were standing at their front gate and looking out at the street, they still didn't know that a playmate was actually so close. As they stood there, wondering what to do and whether anything fun was going to happen that day, or whether it was going to be one of those boring days when they couldn't think of anything to do—just at that moment the gate to Villa Villekulla opened and a little girl came out. She was the strangest girl that Tommy and Annika had ever seen. It was Pippi Longstocking, going out for her morning walk.

This is what she looked like:

Her hair was the color of a carrot and it was braided in two tight braids that stuck straight out. Her nose was the shape of a very small potato, and it was completely covered with freckles. Under her nose was an exceptionally wide mouth with nice white teeth. Her dress was quite odd. Pippi had made it herself. It was supposed to have been blue, but there hadn't been enough blue material, so Pippi had decided to sew on little red patches here and there. On her long, thin legs she wore long stockings, one of them brown and the other black. And she wore black shoes that were exactly twice the length of her feet.

Her father had bought those shoes for her in South America, big enough so she would have room to grow into them, and Pippi never wanted any others.

What made Tommy and Annika really open their eyes wide was the monkey who was sitting on the strange girl's shoulder. It was a little African monkey, and he was dressed in blue pants, a yellow jacket, and a white straw hat.

Pippi set off up the street. She walked with one foot on the sidewalk and the other in the gutter. Tommy and Annika fixed their eyes on her for as long as they could see her. After a while she came back.

Now
she was
walking
backward.

That was so she didn't have to turn around when she came home.

As she reached the gate to Tommy and Annika's house, she stopped. The children looked at each other in silence.

Finally Tommy said, "Why were you walking backward?"

"Why was I walking backward?" said Pippi. "Don't we live in a free country? Can't a person walk any way she likes? Besides, I can tell you that in Egypt everyone walks like that, and nobody thinks there's anything odd about it."

"How do you know that?" asked Tommy. "You've never been to Egypt, have you?"

"Have I been to Egypt! Oh yes, you can bet that I have. I've been everywhere on the whole planet, and I've seen things that are much odder than people walking backward. I wonder what you would have said if I'd walked

16

on my hands, like people do in Farthest India."

"Now you're lying," said Tommy.

Pippi thought for a moment.

"Yes, you're right. I was lying," she said sadly.

"It's bad to lie," said Annika, finally opening her mouth.

"Yes, it's *very* bad to lie," said Pippi, sounding even sadder. "But sometimes I forget, you see. And how can you really expect a little girl whose mamma is an angel and whose pappa is king of the natives—a girl who has sailed the seas all her life—how can you expect her always to tell the truth? And besides," she said, her whole freckled face beaming, "let me tell you that in the Congo there isn't a single person who tells the truth. They tell lies all day long. They start at seven o'clock in the morning and keep on going until sunset. So if I happen to lie once in a while, you'll have to try to forgive me and remember that it's just because I've spent a little too much time in the Congo. But we can still be friends, can't we?"

"Of course," said Tommy, and he suddenly thought that this was probably not going to be one of those boring kind of days.

"So is there anything stopping you from coming to have breakfast at my house?" said Pippi.

"No, of course not," said Tommy. "What would stop us? Come on, let's go!"

"Yes," said Annika. "Let's go!"

"But first I have to introduce you to Mr. Nilsson," said Pippi. And the little monkey took off his hat to greet them politely.

Then they walked through Villa Villekulla's ramshackle front gate and along the gravel path that was lined with old moss-covered trees—they looked like truly splendid climbing trees—and up onto the porch. There stood the horse, munching oats from a soup tureen.

"Why on earth do you have a horse on the porch?" asked Tommy. All the horses he knew about lived in stables.

"Hmm . . ." said Pippi, giving it some thought. "Well, in the kitchen he would just get in the way. And he doesn't feel comfortable in the living room."

Tommy and Annika patted the horse and then

went into the house. There was a kitchen and a living room and a bedroom. But it looked as if Pippi had forgotten to do her Friday cleaning. Tommy and Annika peered around cautiously, just in case the king of the natives happened to be sitting in a corner. They had never in their lives met a king of the natives. But there was no father in sight, nor any mother either.

Annika asked anxiously, "Do you live here all alone?"

"Of course not," said Pippi. "Mr. Nilsson and the horse live here too."

"Yes, but, I mean, isn't there any mother or father here?"

"No, not one," said Pippi cheerfully.

"But who tells you to go to bed at night and things like that?" asked Annika.

"I do," said Pippi. "First I tell myself once, very nicely, and if I don't obey, then I tell myself again, very sternly, and if I still don't obey, then it's time for a spanking, of course."

Tommy and Annika didn't really understand all

this, but they thought it might not be such a bad way of doing things.

By now they were in the kitchen, and Pippi hollered:

"Now it's time to
make **Pancakes**,

now it's time to
flip **Panclips**,

now it's time to
shape **Panchapes**!"

And then she got out three eggs and tossed them high in the air. One of the eggs landed on her head and cracked open, making the yolk run into her eyes. But the other two she easily caught with a saucepan. They smashed into bits in the pan.

"I've always heard that egg yolks are good for your hair," said Pippi, wiping her eyes. "Just wait and see, my hair is going to start growing like mad.

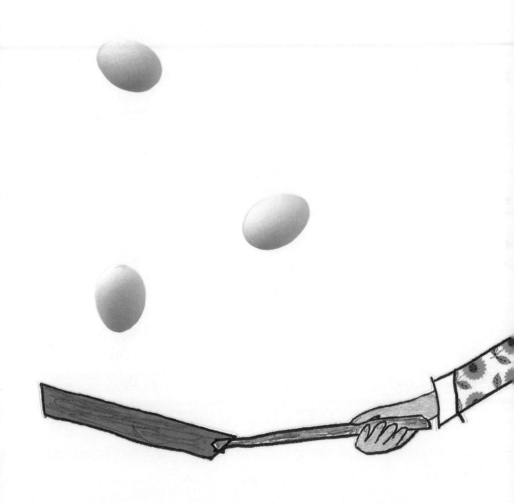

"By the way, in Brazil everyone walks around with egg in their hair. And nobody is bald there, either. Except once there was an old man who was so foolish that he ate up all his eggs instead of smearing them on his hair. And of course he went bald. Whenever he went out on the street, he caused such a commotion that the police cars had to be called out."

While she was talking Pippi nimbly picked the eggshells out of the saucepan with her fingers. Then she took down a bath-brush that was hanging on the wall and started stirring the pancake batter so hard that it splattered all over the walls. Finally she poured what was left onto a griddle that stood on the stove. When the pancake was done on one side, she tossed it halfway up to the ceiling to flip it in the air and then caught it on the griddle. And when the pancake was done, she flung it across the kitchen right onto a plate that was sitting on the table.

"Eat," she cried. "Eat, before it gets cold!"

So Tommy and Annika ate, and they thought it was a very good pancake. Afterward Pippi invited them into the living room. There was only one piece of furniture in the room. It was a very big cabinet with lots of little drawers. Pippi opened the drawers and showed Tommy and Annika all the treasures she kept inside. There were strange birds' eggs, peculiar seashells and stones, elegant little boxes, beautiful silver mirrors, pearl necklaces, and many other things that Pippi and her father had bought on their travels around the world. Pippi gave each of her new playmates a present as a souvenir. She gave Tommy a dagger with a gleaming mother-of-pearl handle, and she gave Annika a little box whose lid was covered with pink seashells. Inside the box was a ring with a green stone.

"Now you'd better go home," said Pippi, "so that you can come back tomorrow. Because if you don't go home, then you won't be able to come back tomorrow. And that would really be a shame."

Tommy and Annika thought so too. And so they went home. They walked past the horse, who had eaten up all the oats, and out through the front gate of Villa Villekulla. Mr. Nilsson waved his hat as they left.

Chapter Two

Pippi Is a Thing-Searcher and Ends Up in a Fight

Annika woke early the next morning. She quickly hopped out of bed and tiptoed over to Tommy.

"Wake up, Tommy," she said, shaking him by the arm. "Wake up. Let's go over and see that funny girl with the big shoes!"

Tommy was instantly wide awake.

"When I was lying here asleep I knew something fun was going to happen today, even though I couldn't remember what it was," he said as he pulled off his pajama top.

Then they both headed for the bathroom. They brushed their teeth and washed much faster than usual. They threw on their clothes. And a whole hour earlier than their mother expected, they came sliding

down the banister. They landed right at the breakfast table, where they sat down and began shouting that they wanted their hot cocoa at once.

"What's going on?" asked their mother. "Why are you in such a hurry?"

"We're going over to see the new girl in the house next door," said Tommy.

"We might stay there all day," said Annika.

On that particular morning, Pippi was in the middle of baking gingersnaps. She had made a huge batch of dough and rolled it out on the kitchen floor.

"Because you know what?" said Pippi to her little monkey. "What good is it to roll the dough on a table when you're going to bake at least five hundred gingersnaps?"

So there she lay on the floor, cutting out heart-shaped gingersnaps for dear life.

"Stop walking in the dough, Mr. Nilsson," she said, sounding annoyed, just as the doorbell rang.

Pippi jumped up to open the door. She was as white as a miller from head to toe, and when she eagerly shook hands with Tommy and Annika, a whole cloud of flour descended on them.

"How nice of you to drop in," she said, shaking out her apron and making another cloud of flour. Tommy and Annika got so much flour in their throats that they had to cough.

"What are you doing?" asked Tommy.

"Well, if I told you that I'm cleaning the chimney, I'm sure you wouldn't believe me, since you're as sharp as a tack," said Pippi. "The fact is that I'm baking. But I'll be finished soon. You can sit on the firewood box to wait."

Pippi could certainly work fast! Tommy and Annika sat down on the firewood box to watch. She rolled out the gingersnap dough, she tossed cookies onto the baking sheets, and she flung the baking sheets into the oven. They thought it was almost like watching a film.

"Done," said Pippi finally, as she slammed the oven door on the last baking sheets with a bang.

"What should we do now?" said Tommy.

"I don't know what you've got in mind," said Pippi, "but I'm not the sort to lie around. I'm a **thing-searcher**, you see. And that means I never have a moment to spare."

"What did you say you were?" asked Annika.

"A **thing-searcher**."

"What's that?" asked Tommy.

"Someone who goes searching for things, of course! What else would it be?" said Pippi as she swept all the flour on the floor into a little pile. "The whole world is full of things, which means there's a real need for someone to go searching for them. And that's exactly what a **thing-searcher** does."

"What kind of things?" asked Annika.

"Oh, all kinds," said Pippi. "Gold nuggets and ostrich feathers and dead mice and tiny little nuts and bolts and things like that."

Tommy and Annika thought this sounded like it might be fun, and they wanted to be thing-searchers too, even though Tommy said that he hoped he would find a gold nugget and not just a tiny little bolt.

"We'll have to wait and see what turns up," said Pippi. "I always find something. But now we'd better hurry before some other **thing-searchers** show up and make off with all the gold nuggets around here."

All three thing-searchers set off. They thought it would be best to search around the nearby houses, because Pippi said that even though it was possible to find little nuts and bolts deep in the woods, the best things were almost always found where people lived.

"Although for that matter," she said, "I've also seen examples of the opposite. I remember one time when I was out searching for things in the jungles of Borneo. There, right in the middle of the primeval forest, where no human being had ever set foot, what do you think I found? A nice wooden leg! Later I gave it away to an old man with only one leg, and he said that all the money in the world couldn't buy a wooden leg like that."

Tommy and Annika watched Pippi to see how a thing-searcher was supposed to act. Pippi ran from one side of the road to the other, shading her eyes with her hand, as she searched and searched. Sometimes she would crawl on her knees, stick her hand between the slats of a fence, and then say with disappointment, "How strange! I was *sure* I saw a gold nugget."

"Can we really take anything that we find?" asked Annika.

"Yes, anything lying on the ground," said Pippi.

Some distance away an old man was lying on the grass outside his house, sleeping.

"That man over there is lying on the ground," said Pippi. "And we found him. So let's take him!"

Tommy and Annika were both quite startled.

"Oh, no, Pippi. We can't take an old man. We just can't," said Tommy. "Besides, what would we do with him?"

"What would we do with him? There are plenty of things we could do. We could put him in a little rabbit cage instead of a rabbit, and feed him dandelion leaves. But if you don't want to, that's fine with me. Even though I think it's annoying that some other **thing-searcher** might come along and nab him."

They kept on going. Suddenly Pippi gave a loud roar.

"Well, I've certainly never seen anything like this," she shouted, and she picked up a big rusty can from the grass. "What a find, what a real *find*! You can never have too many cans."

Tommy looked at the can rather suspiciously and said, "What can you use that for?"

"Oh, you can use this for plenty of things," said Pippi. "For instance, you can put cookies inside it. Then it becomes a nice Can With Cookies. Or you can *not* put cookies inside it. Then it becomes a Can Without Cookies. Of course that's not nearly as nice, but it's still a good thing."

She inspected the can, which was certainly very rusty. It also had a hole in the bottom.

"It looks like this must be a Can Without Cookies,"

she said, giving it some thought. "But you can also put it over your head and pretend that it's the middle of the night."

And that's what she did. With the can over her head she wandered through the neighborhood like some sort of tin tower, and she didn't stop until she tripped over a wire fence and landed flat on her stomach. There was a huge bang when the can hit the ground.

"So there you see," said Pippi, taking off the can. "If I hadn't had this on, I would have landed flat on my face and really hurt myself."

"Yes, but if you hadn't had that can on your head," said Annika, "you would never have tripped over the wire fence."

But before she had even finished speaking, Pippi gave out another roar and triumphantly held up an empty spool of thread.

"This seems to be my lucky day," she said. "Such a sweet, sweet little spool for blowing soap bubbles, or you could put it on a string and wear it like a necklace! I'm going to go home and do that right now."

At that very moment the gate of a nearby house flew open and a boy came rushing out. He looked scared, which wasn't so strange, because right on his heels were five other boys. They soon caught him and then shoved him against a fence, where they all attacked him. All five of them started hitting and punching him. He began to cry, and held up his arms to shield his face.

"Go to it, boys," yelled the biggest and strongest of the lot. "That way he'll never dare show his face on this street again!"

"Oh," said Annika. "That's Willy they're beating up. How can they be so mean!"

"It's that horrible Bengt. He's always fighting," said Tommy. "But five against one—what cowards!"

Pippi went over to the boys and tapped Bengt on the back with her finger.

"Hey there," she said. "Are you planning to make mincemeat out of little Willy, since all five of you are going at him at once?"

Bengt turned around and caught sight of a girl he had never seen before. A complete stranger who dared to poke him. At first he merely stared at her, out of sheer astonishment, but then a big sneer appeared on his face.

"Boys," he said. "Boys! Forget about Willy and take a look at this girl. What a weird little girl she is!"

He slapped his knees and started laughing. In a flash they were all crowding around Pippi, all except for Willy, who wiped away his tears and timidly went over to stand next to Tommy.

"Look at that hair of hers! Bright as fire! And those shoes," Bengt went on. "Could I borrow one of them? I really want to go out rowing, but I don't have a boat."

Then he grabbed one of Pippi's braids, but dropped it instantly and said, "Ow, I burned myself!"

And then all five of the boys who were standing around Pippi started jumping and shouting, "Flare-hair, flare-hair!"

Pippi stood in the middle of the circle and smiled in a friendly way. Bengt was hoping that she would get mad or start to cry. At the very least she should look scared. But when nothing else seemed to work, he gave her a shove.

"I don't think you have a very nice way of treating ladies," said Pippi. And then she lifted him up in her strong arms, high up in the air. She carried him over to a birch tree that stood nearby and slung him over a branch. Then she picked up the second boy and hung him over another branch. And she took the next one and set him on top of the gatepost outside a house. The next one she tossed over a fence so that he ended up sitting in a flowerbed in a nearby garden. And the last of the bullies she put in a tiny little toy wagon that was standing on the road. Then Pippi and Tommy and Annika and Willy all stood there for a moment, looking at the boys, who were speechless with surprise.

Pippi said, "What cowards you are! It takes all five of you to attack one boy. How cowardly. And then you start shoving around a defenseless little girl too. That's really awful!"

To Tommy and Annika she said, "Come on, let's go home." And to Willy she said, "Just come and tell me if they ever try to beat you up again."

To Bengt, who was perched up in the tree and didn't dare move, she said, "If you have anything else to say about my hair or my shoes, it'd be best if you told me now, before I go home."

But Bengt had nothing more to say about Pippi's shoes, or about her hair either. Then Pippi picked up the can in one hand and the spool in the other and went on her way, followed by Tommy and Annika.

When they reached Pippi's garden, Pippi said, "Oh dear, how annoying! Here I've found two such fine things, and you've found nothing. You'll have to search a little harder. Tommy, why don't you look inside that old tree? Old trees are some of the best places for a thing-searcher to look."

Tommy said that he didn't think he and Annika were ever going to find anything, but to please Pippi he stuck his hand into a hollow in the tree trunk.

"Wait a minute," he said in astonishment, and pulled out his hand. And in it he was holding a truly splendid notebook with a leather cover. In a special holder was a little silver pen.

"Now that's really strange," said Tommy.

"You see?" said Pippi. "There's nothing as great as being a thing-searcher. It's odd that more people don't take up the profession. They all want to be carpenters and shoemakers and chimneysweeps and stuff like that, but thing-searchers—no thank you, that's not good enough for them!"

And then she looked at Annika.

"Why don't you go and feel around inside that

old stump? There are almost always things to be found inside old stumps."

Annika stuck her hand inside, and almost at once she found a red coral necklace. Then she and Tommy just stood there gaping for a long time, they were so surprised. And they thought that from now on they were going to be thing-searchers every single day.

Pippi had been up half the night playing catch, and now she suddenly felt sleepy.

"I think I'd better go and lie down for a while," she said. "Why don't you come along and tuck me in?"

When Pippi sat down on the edge of her bed and took off her shoes, she thought for a moment and then said, "That Bengt said he was going out rowing. Phooey!" She snickered scornfully. "I'll teach him to row, yes I will! Just wait until next time!"

"Tell me, Pippi," said Tommy in a respectful tone of voice, "why do you have such big shoes?"

"So I can wiggle my toes, of course," she replied. Then she lay down to sleep. She always slept with her feet on the pillow and her head under the covers.

"They sleep like this in Guatemala," she assured

them. "It's the only proper way to sleep. And this way I can wiggle my toes while I'm sleeping too.

"Can you fall asleep without a lullaby?" she went on. "I always have to sing to myself for a while, otherwise I can't sleep a wink all night."

Tommy and Annika listened to the humming sound coming from under the covers. Pippi was singing herself to sleep. Carefully and quietly they tiptoed out of the room so as not to disturb her. In the doorway they turned around and cast one last glance at the bed. They could see nothing but Pippi's feet, resting on the pillow. There she lay, briskly wiggling her toes.

Then Tommy and Annika ran home. Annika was clutching her coral necklace tightly in her hand.

"Well, that was really very odd," she said. "Tommy, you don't think that . . . you don't think that Pippi put these things there beforehand, do you?"

"You never know," said Tommy. "You never really know anything when it comes to Pippi Longstocking."

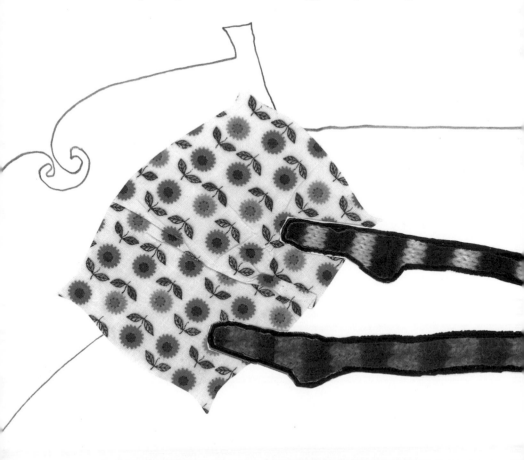

Chapter Three

Pippi Plays Tag with the Police

Soon everyone in that little town knew that a nine-year-old girl was living alone in Villa Villekulla. The grown-ups in town, both the men and the women, did not approve in the least. All children needed to have someone to scold them, and all children needed to go to school and learn the multiplication tables. And that's why all the grown-ups decided that the little girl in Villa Villekulla should be sent to a children's home at once.

One beautiful afternoon Pippi had
invited Tommy and Annika to come over
for coffee and gingersnaps. She had set out
the coffee tray on the porch steps. It was
sunny and lovely out there, and all the
flowers in Pippi's garden were so fragrant.

Mr. Nilsson kept climbing around
on the porch railing. And now
and then the horse would
stick out his nose for a
gingersnap.

"Oh, how glorious it is to be
alive," said Pippi, stretching
out her legs as far as they
would go.

43

Right at that moment, two policemen in full uniform came striding through the gate.

"Wow," said Pippi. "This must be another lucky day for me. Policemen are the best thing I can think of. Except for rhubarb pudding, of course."

And she walked over to greet the policemen, her face beaming with delight.

"Are you the girl who has moved into Villa Villekulla?" one of the officers asked her.

"Far from it," said Pippi. "I'm a tiny little woman who lives in a third-floor apartment at the other end of town."

She just said that because she felt like teasing the policemen a little. But they didn't think it was the least bit funny. They said that she shouldn't try to be smart with them. And then they told her that all the nice people in town were making arrangements so that she could have a room in a children's home.

"But I already live in a children's home," said Pippi.

"What's that? Has it already been arranged?" asked one of the officers. "Where is this children's home?"

44

"Here," said Pippi proudly. "I'm a child, and this is my home, so it's a children's home. And I have room here, plenty of room."

"My dear child," said the policeman with a smile, "you don't understand. You have to go to a real children's home where somebody can look after you."

"Are horses allowed in your children's home?" asked Pippi.

"No, of course not," said the officer.

"I was afraid of that," said Pippi, sounding gloomy. "Well, what about monkeys?"

"Certainly not. I'm sure you realize that."

"I see," said Pippi. "Then you're going to have to look somewhere else to find kids for your children's home. I have no intention of moving there."

"Yes, but don't you realize that you have to go to school?" said the policeman.

"Why do I have to go to school?"

"To learn things, of course."

"What sort of things?" asked Pippi.

"All kinds of things," said the officer. "Lots of useful things, like the multiplication tables, for instance."

"I've been fine for nine years without any **pluttification** tables," said Pippi. "And I'm sure I can manage in the future, too."

"Yes, but think how sad it will be for you to be so ignorant. What about when you grow up and someone happens to ask you what the capital of Portugal is and you can't answer?"

"Of course I can answer," said Pippi. "I'll just answer like this: If you're so desperately anxious to know what the capital of Portugal is, then by all means write a letter to Portugal and ask them!"

"But don't you think you'd feel silly that you couldn't answer the question yourself?"

"That's possible. Occasionally I might lie awake at night and wonder over and over: What on earth is the capital of Portugal? But you can't expect that things will always be fun," said Pippi, as she went into a handstand and stayed there for a moment. "Besides, I've been to Lisbon with my pappa," she went on as she stood upside down, because that didn't stop her from talking.

But then one of the officers said that Pippi certainly shouldn't go around thinking that she could do whatever she liked. She was going to have to come with them to the children's home, right then and there. He walked toward her and grabbed her by the arm. But Pippi quickly tore herself loose, gave him a light tap, and said, "You're It!"

Before he could even blink, she had leaped up onto the porch railing. With a couple of bounds she was up on the balcony above the porch. The policemen had no desire to climb up the same way. So they dashed inside the house and up to the second floor. But by the time they came out onto the balcony, Pippi was already halfway up the roof. She climbed across the shingles as if she were a monkey. In a flash she reached the ridge and then nimbly jumped up onto the chimney. On the balcony below, the police officers were scratching their heads, and on the lawn stood Tommy and Annika, peering up at Pippi.

"This is so much *fun* playing tag," cried Pippi. "And it was nice of you to come to visit. This *is* my lucky day today, I can feel it."

After the policemen had pondered things for a moment, they went to get a ladder, which they propped against one end of the house. Then they climbed up, one after the other, planning to bring Pippi back down. But they looked a little scared as they climbed out on the ridge of the roof and started teetering their way toward Pippi.

"Don't be scared," called Pippi. "It's not dangerous. It's fun."

When the policemen were within two paces of Pippi, she quickly hopped down from the chimney and, shrieking and laughing, she ran along the ridge to the other end of the house. A couple of yards from the house stood a tree.

"Now it's time for a

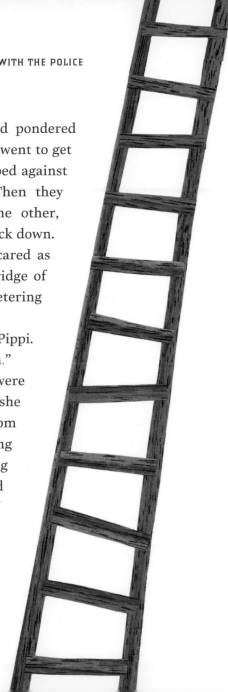

dive," yelled Pippi, and then she jumped straight down into the green crown of the tree. She hung on to a branch, dangled back and forth for a moment, and let herself drop to the ground. Then she darted over to the other end of the house and took away the ladder.

The policemen looked a bit dismayed when Pippi jumped, but they were even more dismayed when they teetered their way back along the ridge to climb down the ladder. At first they were terribly angry. They yelled at Pippi, who was standing down below peering up at them. They told her to bring the ladder back at once or she was going to be in real trouble.

"Why are you so angry?" asked Pippi reproachfully. "We're just playing a game of tag. Why not be friends?"

The officers thought about this for a moment, and at last one of them said, sounding embarrassed, "Er . . . listen to me, would you be kind enough to put back the ladder so we can get down?"

"Of course I will," said Pippi, and she instantly put

back the ladder. "And then why don't we drink some coffee and have a nice time?"

But those officers were awfully sly, because as soon as they reached the ground, they rushed at Pippi, shouting, "We're going to get you now, you horrid little beast!"

But then Pippi said, "No, I don't have time to play anymore. But it certainly has been fun, I'll admit that."

And she took a firm grip on the belts of both policemen and carried them down the garden path, through the gate, and out to the street. There she set them down, and it took a long time for them to pull themselves together and get to their feet.

"Wait a minute," called Pippi, and then she ran into the kitchen. She came out with a couple of heart-shaped gingersnaps and said pleasantly, "Would you like one? You don't mind if they're a little burned, do you?"

Then she went back to Tommy and Annika, who were standing there with their eyes wide, completely astonished. The policemen hurried back to town, and they told all the grown-ups, both the men and the women, that Pippi wasn't really suited to a children's home. They didn't mention that they had been up on the roof. And the grown-ups thought it might be best to allow Pippi to continue living at Villa Villekulla. If she wanted to go to school, then she could make her own arrangements.

But Pippi and Tommy and Annika had a very pleasant afternoon. They went back to their coffee party, which had been interrupted.

Pippi devoured fourteen gingersnaps, and then she said, "Those two are not my idea of what real policemen should be like. Not at all! Far too much talk about children's homes and Lisbon and **pluffification** tables."

Afterward she lifted the horse down from the porch, and all three of them went for a ride. At first Annika was scared and didn't want to go, but when she saw how much fun Tommy and Pippi were having, she let Pippi lift her up onto the horse's back too. And the horse trotted around and around the garden while Tommy sang, "Here come the Swedes, with a clatter and clang!"

After Tommy and Annika had crawled into bed that evening, Tommy said, "Annika, don't you think it's great that Pippi moved here?"

"Of course I do," said Annika.

"I can't even remember what games we used to play before she came here. Can you?"

"Hmm . . . we played croquet and things like that," said Annika. "But I think it's much more fun with Pippi. And with the horse and everything else!"

Chapter Four

Pippi Goes to School

Tommy and Annika went to school, of course. Every morning at eight o'clock they would trudge off, hand in hand, with their schoolbooks under their arms.

At that time of day Pippi would usually be grooming her horse or getting Mr. Nilsson dressed in his little suit. Or else she would be doing her morning exercises, which involved standing up straight and then doing forty-three somersaults, one after another. Afterward she would sit on the kitchen table and in blissful silence drink a big cup of coffee and eat a cheese sandwich.

Tommy and Annika would always cast a longing glance at Villa Villekulla as they plodded off to school. They would much rather have gone over to play with Pippi. At least if Pippi went to school too, things would have been better.

"Just think how much fun we could have together when we walked home from school," said Tommy.

"Yes, and on the way there too," Annika added.

The more they thought about it, the sadder it seemed to them that Pippi didn't go to school. Finally they decided to try to convince her to start.

"You have no idea what a nice teacher we have," Tommy slyly told Pippi one afternoon when he and Annika went over to Villa Villekulla after they had finished all their homework.

"If you only knew how much *fun* it is at school," Annika assured her. "I'd go crazy if I weren't allowed to go."

Pippi was sitting on a stool, in the middle of washing her feet in a basin. She didn't say a word, just wiggled her toes for a moment so that the water splashed all around.

"You don't really have to be there very long," Tommy went on. "Only till two o'clock."

"That's right, and then you get Christmas vacation and Easter vacation and summer vacation," said Annika.

Pippi bit her big toe as she gave this some thought, but she still didn't say a word. All of a sudden she seemed to make up her mind. She poured all the water out onto the kitchen floor so that Mr. Nilsson, who was sitting nearby and playing with a mirror, got his pants completely soaked.

"It's not fair," said Pippi sternly, not paying any attention to Mr. Nilsson's complaints about his wet pants. "It's absolutely not fair! I don't intend to put up with this!"

"With what?" asked Tommy.

"In four months it will be Christmas, and then you'll have a holiday. But what about me? What do I get?" Pippi sounded sad. "No Christmas vacation, not even a little Christmas vacation," she complained. "Something has to change. Tomorrow I'm going to start school."

Tommy and Annika clapped their hands with glee.

"Hooray! Then we'll wait for you outside our front gate at eight o'clock."

"Oh no," said Pippi. "I can't start that early. And besides, I'm probably going to ride to school."

And she did. At exactly ten o'clock the following day, she lifted her horse down from the porch. A short time later everyone in the little town dashed to the windows to see the horse that had bolted. Or rather, they thought it had bolted. But it hadn't. It was only Pippi, who was in a bit of a hurry to get to school. At full gallop she raced into the playground, leaped off the horse before he even stopped, and tied him to a tree. Then she flung open the door to the classroom with such a bang that Tommy and Annika and all their nice classmates gave a start as they sat at their desks.

"Hey, everybody," hollered Pippi, swinging her big hat. "Am I in time for **pluⱦification**?"

Tommy and Annika had told their teacher that a new girl named Pippi Longstocking was going to be coming. Their teacher had also heard people in the little town talking about Pippi. And because she was a very kind and pleasant teacher, she had decided to do everything she could to make Pippi feel welcome at school.

Pippi flung herself down on an empty chair before anyone even invited her to do so. But the teacher paid no attention to her brash behavior. She merely said in a very friendly voice, "Welcome to school, Pippi dear. I hope that you'll be happy here and that you'll learn a great deal."

"Yes, well, I hope that I'll get a Christmas vacation," said Pippi. "That's why I've come here. Fair's fair, after all!"

"First, if you wouldn't mind giving me your full name," said the teacher. "Then I can register you at school."

"My name is **Pippilotta Comestibles Windowshade**

Curlymint Ephraimsdaughter Longstocking, the daughter of **Captain Ephraim Longstocking,** formerly the terror of the high seas, now king of the natives. Pippi is really just a nickname because Pappa thought that **Pippilotta** was too long to say."

"I see," said the teacher. "All right then, we'll call you Pippi too. But perhaps we should test your knowledge a bit," she went on. "You're a big girl, and I'm sure you already know quite a lot. Perhaps we could start with arithmetic. Now, Pippi, tell me, how much is seven plus five?"

Pippi looked at her, both surprised and annoyed. Then she said, "If you don't know the answer yourself, I have no intention of telling you!"

All the children stared at Pippi in horror. The teacher explained to her that she wasn't allowed to talk back to teachers that way at school. And she was supposed to address the teacher as "Ma'am."

"Please forgive me," Pippi apologized. "I didn't know that. I won't do it again."

"Well, I hope not," said the teacher. "So now I'll tell you that seven plus five equals twelve."

"You see," said Pippi, "you knew it all along. Why did you have to ask me? Oh, what an idiot I am, I forgot to say 'Ma'am' again. Sorry," she said, and then she pinched herself hard on the ear.

The teacher decided to ignore this. She went on, "All right, Pippi. How much do you think eight plus four is?"

"About sixty-seven or so," Pippi guessed.

"Not at all," said the teacher. "Eight plus four equals twelve."

"Now wait a minute, my dear lady, that's going too far," said Pippi. "You just told me that seven plus five equals twelve. I should think there have to be some rules, even in a school. Besides, if you get such childish delight out of silly things like this, why don't you go and sit by yourself in the corner to do arithmetic and leave us in peace so we can play tag? Oh no, now I forgot to say 'Ma'am' again," she cried in horror. "Could you *please* forgive me just one last time? I'll *try* to remember a little better from now on."

The teacher agreed to do this, but she didn't think it was such a good idea to try teaching Pippi any more arithmetic. Instead, she started asking the other children questions.

"Tommy, can you give me the correct answer to this problem?" she said. "If Lisa has seven apples and Axel has nine apples, how many apples do they have all together?"

"Yes, let's hear your answer, Tommy," Pippi piped in. "And at the same time, tell me this: If Lisa has a stomach ache and Axel has an even worse stomach ache, whose fault is it, and where did they swipe those apples from?"

The teacher tried to pretend that she hadn't heard a thing, and she turned to Annika.

"All right, Annika, here's a problem for you: Gustav went on a school outing with his classmates. He had one krona when he left and seven öre when he came home. How much money did he spend?"

"Hey," said Pippi, "I also want to know: Why was he such a spendthrift, and did he buy lemonade with his money, and did he wash behind his ears properly before he left home?"

The teacher decided to give up on arithmetic

altogether. She thought Pippi might like learning to read instead. So she took out a sweet little picture of an iguana. In front of the iguana's nose was the letter "i."

"All right, Pippi, now I'm going to show you something fun," she said briskly. "Here you see an iguana. And this letter in front is an 'i.'"

"Oh no, I don't think so," said Pippi. "I think that looks like a stick with a little fly speck on top. And I'd really like to know what an iguana has to do with a fly speck."

The teacher took out the next picture, which showed a snake, and she told Pippi that the letter in front was an "s."

"peaking of snakes," said Pippi, "I'll never forget the time that I wrestled with a giant snake in India. It was the most horrible snake you could imagine. He was forty feet long and angry as a hornet, and every day he ate five grown Indians, plus two little children for dessert.

64

"Once he wanted to have me for dessert, too, and he wrapped himself around me—*crunch*—but 'I have sailed the seven seas, after all,' I told him, and bonked him on the head—*bam!*—and then he started hissing—$szszszs^zszsz$—so I hit him again—*bam!*—and *poof*—he died. So that's the letter 's.' How amazing!"

Pippi had to pause to catch her breath. And the teacher, who was beginning to think that Pippi was a troublesome and difficult child, suggested that the class should do some drawing instead. Surely Pippi would be able to sit quietly and draw, thought the teacher. She took out paper and pens and passed them out to the children.

"You can draw whatever you like," she said, as she sat down at her desk and started correcting homework. After a while she looked up to see how the drawing was going. All the children were sitting there watching Pippi, who was lying on the floor, drawing to her heart's content.

"Pippi," said the teacher impatiently, "why aren't you drawing on the piece of paper?"

"I filled it up long ago. I couldn't get my horse on that tiny scrap of paper," said Pippi. "Right now I'm drawing his front legs, but when I get to the tail I'll probably have to go out into the hallway."

The teacher thought hard for a moment.

"Why don't we sing a little song instead," she suggested.

All the children stood up next to their desks—all except Pippi, who was still lying on the floor.

"Go ahead and sing," she said. "I'll just rest for a while. All this learning can be too much for even the strongest person."

But now the teacher had lost all patience. She told the other children to go out to the playground, because she wanted to have a private conversation with Pippi.

When the teacher and Pippi were alone, Pippi stood up and went over to the desk.

"You know what?" she said. "I mean . . . er . . . you know what, Ma'am? It was really fun to come here and see what all of you do, but I don't think I feel like coming to school anymore. I'll just have to make do without a Christmas vacation. There are just too many apples and iguanas and snakes and things like that. It makes my head spin. I hope you're not disappointed, Ma'am."

But the teacher said that she did feel disappointed, mainly because Pippi didn't want to try to behave properly, and because a girl who behaved the way Pippi did couldn't be allowed to come to school, no matter how much she might want to.

"Have I behaved badly?" asked Pippi, very surprised. "Oh, and I didn't even know it," she said, looking woeful. Nobody could look as woeful as Pippi when she was sad.

She was silent for a moment, and then she said in a

quavering voice, "You have to understand, Ma'am, that if a girl's mamma is an angel and her pappa is king of the natives and if she herself has spent her whole life sailing the seas, then she doesn't really know how to behave at school among all these apples and iguanas."

Then the teacher said that she understood and that she wasn't annoyed at Pippi anymore and that perhaps Pippi could come back to school when she was a little older.

And then Pippi, beaming with joy, said, "I think you're awfully nice, Ma'am. And here's something for you!"

From her pocket Pippi took out an elegant little gold watch, which she placed on the desk. The teacher said that she couldn't accept such an expensive gift.

But Pippi said, "You have to! Otherwise I'll come back tomorrow, and then there will really be a commotion."

After that Pippi dashed out to the playground and leaped onto her horse. All the children crowded around her to pat the horse and see her off.

"Give me the schools in Argentina any time," said Pippi, sounding a bit haughty as she looked down at the children. "You should try going there.

Easter vacation starts only three days after Christmas vacation ends, and when Easter vacation is over, there are three days until summer vacation starts. Summer vacation ends on the first of November, and then, of course, it's quite a while before Christmas vacation starts on November eleventh. But it's bearable because at least there's no homework. It's strictly forbidden to do homework in Argentina. Sometimes an Argentinean boy might sneak into a cupboard and sit there and secretly do homework, but I feel sorry for him if his mother finds out. They don't have any arithmetic in the schools there. If anyone knows how much seven plus five is, and if he's silly enough to mention it to the teacher, he has to stand in the corner all day long. Reading is something they do only on Fridays, and then only if they have some books to read. But they never do."

"Well, what do they do at school then?" asked a little boy.

"They eat candy," said Pippi firmly. "There's a long pipe that goes from the nearby candy factory straight to the classroom, and candy comes gushing out all day long, so the kids can hardly keep up with eating it."

"But what does the teacher do?" asked a girl.

"She unwraps the candy for the children, silly," said Pippi. "You don't really think they do that themselves, do you? Hardly! And they don't actually go to school themselves either. They send their brothers."

Pippi swung her big hat.

"Bye now, kids," she shouted happily. "You won't be seeing me for a while, but don't ever forget how many apples Axel had or you'll be sorry. Ha ha ha!"

With a resounding laugh, Pippi rode out through the gate, making the gravel fly under the horse's hooves and rattling the windowpanes of the school.

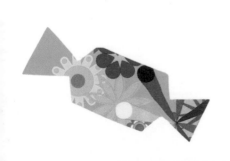

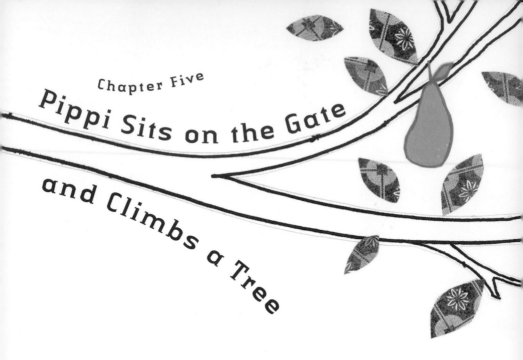

Chapter Five
Pippi Sits on the Gate
and Climbs a Tree

Outside Villa Villekulla sat Pippi, Tommy, and Annika. Pippi was sitting on one of the gateposts, and Annika was on the other, while Tommy was sitting on the gate itself. It was a warm and beautiful day in late August. A pear tree that stood very close to the gate stretched its branches so far down that the children could sit there and pick the best little yellow-and-red August pears without much trouble at all. They munched and crunched, spitting the seeds out onto the road.

Villa Villekulla stood just where the little town ended and the countryside began, and where the street turned into a country road. The people in the little town were very fond of taking a stroll out toward Villa Villekulla, because that was the prettiest area of all.

Just as the children were sitting there eating pears, a girl came walking down the road from town. When she caught sight of the children she stopped and asked, "Have you seen my pappa go past?"

"Hmm," said Pippi. "What does he look like? Does he have blue eyes?"

"Yes," said the girl.

"About average height, not too tall and not too short?"

"Yes," said the girl.

"A black hat and black shoes?"

"Yes, that's right," said the girl eagerly.

"Nope, we haven't seen him," said Pippi firmly.

The girl looked disappointed and started off without another word.

"Wait a minute," Pippi called after her. "Is he bald?"

"No, he certainly is not," said the girl angrily.

"Lucky for him," said Pippi as she spit out a seed.

The girl was now in a hurry to leave, but then Pippi shouted, "Does he have unnaturally big ears that reach all the way down to his shoulders?"

"No," said the girl, turning around in surprise. "Surely you don't mean that you've seen a man walk past here with big ears like that?"

"I've never seen anyone walk with his ears," said Pippi. "Everyone I know walks with his feet."

"Ugh, how stupid you are. I mean, have you really seen a man who has such big ears?"

"Well, no," said Pippi. "Nobody has big ears like that. That would be absurd. And how would it look? Nobody should have ears as big as that. At least not in this country," she added after giving it some thought. "In China things are a little different, you know. I once saw a Chinese man in Shanghai. His ears were so big that he used them as a cloak. Whenever it rained he would just crawl in under his ears, and that was the warmest and best place to be. Although it wasn't so nice for his ears, of course. If the weather was especially bad, he used to invite his friends and acquaintances to camp out under his ears. There they would sit, singing their melancholy songs, until the storm had passed. They were all very fond of him because of his ears. Hai Shang was his name. You should have seen Hai Shang dashing off to work in the morning! He would always come running at the last minute because he was so fond of sleeping late in the morning, and you can't imagine how sweet it looked when he came rushing up with his ears

75

fluttering behind him like two big yellow sails."

The girl had stopped and was standing there with her mouth open, listening to Pippi. And Tommy and Annika had lost interest in eating more pears. They were too busy listening to the story.

"He had more children than he could count, and the youngest one was named Peter," said Pippi.

"Oh, but a Chinese child can't be called Peter," Tommy objected.

"That was exactly what his wife told him. 'A Chinese child can't be called Peter,' she said. But Hai Shang was terribly stubborn, and he said that either the child would be named Peter or nothing at all. And then he sat down in a corner and pulled his ears over his head and sulked. So his poor wife had to give in, of course, and the boy was named Peter."

"Really?" said Annika.

"He was the most troublesome child in all of Shanghai," Pippi went on. "He was so fussy about his food that he made his mamma very unhappy. Now, you do know that they eat birds' nests in China, don't you? So there sat his mamma with a whole plate of

birds' nests, trying to feed him. 'All right, little
Peter,' she said, 'let's eat a bird's nest for Pappa!' But
Peter just pressed his lips together and shook
his head. Finally Hai Shang got so mad at his son that
he said no new food would be cooked for Peter until
he ate a bird's nest for Pappa. And when Hai
Shang said something, that was how it had
to be. That same bird's nest went back and
forth from the kitchen from May until meatballs
October. On the fourteenth of July Peter's
mamma begged to be allowed to give him a
couple of   , but Hai Shang said no."

"Nonsense," said the girl in the road.

"Yes, that's exactly what Hai Shang said," Pippi
went on. "'Nonsense,' he said. 'It's obvious that the
boy could eat the bird's nest if he'd only stop being so
stubborn.' But Peter just pressed his lips together the
whole time, from May till October."

"But how could he stay alive?" asked Tommy in
astonishment.

"He couldn't stay alive," said Pippi. "He died. From
pure stubbornness. On the eighteenth of October.

And he was buried on the nineteenth. On the twentieth a swallow came flying through the window and laid eggs in the bird's nest that was sitting on the table. So at least it was put to good use. No harm done," said Pippi merrily. Then she gazed thoughtfully at the girl who was standing there, looking bewildered.

"You've certainly got an odd look on your face," said Pippi. "What's the matter? Surely you don't think that I'm sitting here telling lies, do you? Excuse me? Just tell me if that's what you think," said Pippi ominously as she pushed up her sleeves.

"No, no, not at all," said the girl, sounding scared. "I wouldn't exactly say that you were lying, but . . ."

"You wouldn't, huh?" said Pippi. "Well, that's precisely what I *am* doing. I'm lying so much that my tongue has turned black—can't you tell? Do you really think that a boy could live without food from May till October? All right, I know he could manage without food for three or four months or so, but from May to October? That's just plain nonsense. Surely you realize that it has to be a lie. You really shouldn't believe everything people tell you."

Then the girl took off, and she didn't turn around again.

"Some people really are gullible," Pippi said to Tommy and Annika. "From May till October! How stupid can you be!"

Then she yelled after the girl, "No, we haven't seen your pappa! We haven't seen a *single* bald man all day long. But yesterday seventeen of them went by. Arm in arm!"

Pippi's garden was truly delightful. It was not well kept—no, it wasn't. But it had glorious lawns that were never mowed and old rosebushes full of white and yellow and pink roses. They may not have been particularly elegant, of course, but they had such a lovely scent. A good many fruit trees grew there too, and—best of all—several ancient oak and elm trees that were perfect for climbing.

Tommy and Annika's garden had very few climbing trees, and their mother was always so afraid that they would fall and hurt themselves. That's why they hadn't done much climbing so far.

But now Pippi said, "Why don't we climb that oak tree over there?"

Tommy instantly jumped down from the gate, delighted at the suggestion. Annika was a bit more cautious, but when she saw that there were big burls sticking out of the trunk that could be used as steps, she too thought it would be fun to try.

A couple of yards above the ground the oak split into two, and right at the spot where it split there was a small flat space. It didn't take long before all three children were sitting up there. Above their heads the oak spread out its crown like a green roof.

"This would be a good place to drink coffee," said Pippi. "I'll just run into the house and make us a pot."

Tommy and Annika clapped their hands and shouted, "Yippee!"

It didn't take long
before Pippi had the coffee
ready. And she had baked rolls the day before.
She took up a position at the foot of the oak tree
and started tossing up coffee cups. Tommy and
Annika caught them. But sometimes it was
the oak that caught them, and two coffee cups
broke. Pippi ran back to the house for more.
Then it was the rolls' turn, and for a long
time there was a shower of rolls in the air.
At least they didn't break. Finally Pippi

climbed up, holding the
coffeepot in one hand. She
also brought cream in a bottle
and sugar in a little box.

Tommy and Annika thought that coffee had
never tasted so good before. They weren't allowed
to drink coffee every day, only when they were
invited out. And now they had been invited out.
Annika spilled a little coffee on her lap. At first it was
hot and wet, and then it was cold and wet, but Annika
said that it didn't matter.

When they were finished, Pippi tossed the cups down to the lawn.

"I want to see if the china they make these days is very sturdy," she said. Strangely enough, one cup and all three plates survived intact. The coffeepot lost only its spout.

Then Pippi decided to climb a little higher up the tree.

"Have you ever seen such a thing?" she shouted suddenly. "This tree is hollow!"

There was a big hole in the trunk. The leaves had hidden it from the children's view.

"Oh, can I climb up and see it too?" said Tommy. But there was no answer. "Pippi, where are you?" he shouted uneasily.

Then they heard Pippi's voice, but it wasn't coming from above. It was far below them. It sounded as if it came from underground.

"I'm inside the tree. It's hollow all the way down to the ground. If I peek out through a little crack, I can see the coffeepot lying on the grass outside."

"But how are you going to get back up?" cried Annika.

"I'm never getting back up," said Pippi. "I'm going to stay here until I retire. And you'll have to drop food down to me through the hole up above. Five or six times a day."

Annika started to cry.

"Why weep and moan?" said Pippi. "The two of you should come down here with me. Then we can pretend that we're languishing away in a dungeon."

"Not on your life," said Annika. And for safety's sake she climbed down from the tree altogether.

"Annika, I can see you through the crack," cried Pippi. "Don't step on the coffeepot! It's a nice old coffeepot that has never done anyone any harm. It's not the pot's fault that it doesn't have a spout anymore."

Annika went over to the tree trunk, and through a little crack she could see the very tip of Pippi's index finger. This made her feel a whole lot better, but she was still worried.

"Pippi, is it really true that you can't get back up?" she asked.

Pippi's finger disappeared, and it didn't take even

heard Pippi's voice

Can see you through the tree shook

plates survived intact.

Not on your life,' Pippi said.

The climbed down from the tree

Pippi's voice

out through a

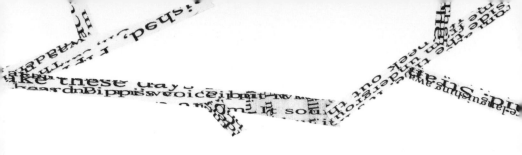

a minute before her face was sticking out of the hole high up in the tree.

"Maybe I can if I really try," she said as she pushed aside the leaves with her hands.

"Is it that easy to climb back up?" said Tommy, who was still up in the tree. "Then I want to try going down inside and languishing for a while."

"All right," said Pippi, "but I think we should get a ladder."

She crawled her way out of the hole and quickly slid down to the ground. Then she ran to get a ladder, which she lugged up into the tree and lowered down into the hole.

Tommy couldn't wait to try it out. It was quite difficult to climb up to the hole because it was high up, but Tommy was brave. And he wasn't afraid to climb down inside the dark tree trunk either. Annika watched him disappear, and she really wondered if she would ever see him again. She tried peeking through the crack.

"Annika," she heard Tommy's voice say. "You wouldn't believe how wonderful it is in here. You really *have* to come inside too. It's not the least bit dangerous if you use a ladder. Once you try it, you won't want to do anything else."

"Are you sure?" said Annika.

"Absolutely," said Tommy.

So with trembling legs Annika climbed back up the tree, and Pippi helped her with the last difficult part. She shrank back a bit when she saw how dark it was inside the trunk, but Pippi held her hand and encouraged her.

"Don't be scared, Annika," she heard Tommy say from below. "I can see your legs now, and I'll be sure to catch you if you fall."

But Annika didn't fall. She climbed down to Tommy safe and sound. And Pippi followed a moment later.

"Isn't this great?" said Tommy.

And Annika had to agree. It wasn't nearly as dark as she had thought, because light was coming in through the crack. Annika went over to see if she too could see the coffeepot on the grass outside.

"This will be our hiding place," said Tommy. "No one will ever know we're in here. And if they go around outside looking for us, we'll be able to watch them through the crack. And then we'll laugh."

"We could get a little twig and poke it through the crack and tickle them," said Pippi. "Then they'll think the tree's haunted."

At this thought the children were so happy that they all hugged each other. Then they heard the gong ringing, which meant that Tommy and Annika had to go home to dinner.

"How stupid," said Tommy. "We have to go home now. But we'll come over tomorrow, as soon as we get home from school."

"Do that," said Pippi.

And then they climbed up the ladder—first Pippi, then Annika, and last of all Tommy. And then they climbed down from the tree—first Pippi, then Annika, and last of all Tommy.

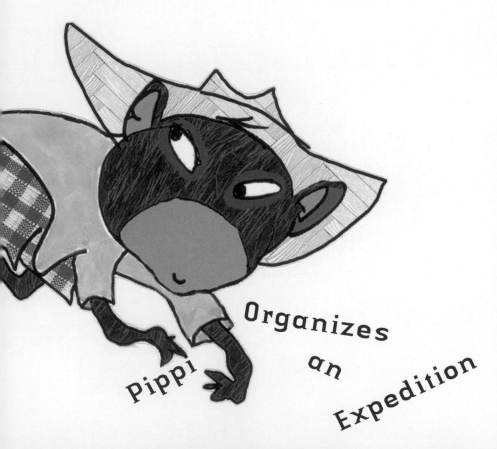

Chapter Six

Pippi Organizes an Expedition

"Today we're not going to school," Tommy told Pippi. "Because it's a house-cleaning holiday."

"Ha!" cried Pippi. "Yet another injustice! I certainly don't get any house-cleaning holiday, not me, no matter how much I might need it. Just look at my kitchen floor! But actually," she added, "when I really think about it, I can clean even without a holiday. And that's what I'm thinking of doing right now, cleaning holiday or no cleaning holiday. I'd like to see somebody try and stop me! Go and sit on the kitchen table so you won't get in the way."

Tommy and Annika obediently climbed up onto the table, and Mr. Nilsson hopped up there too and then lay down to sleep on Annika's lap.

Pippi heated a big kettle of water, which she then emptied onto the kitchen floor. After that she took off her big shoes and placed them neatly on the breadboard. Then she tied two scrub brushes onto her bare feet and began skating all over the floor, making a squishing noise as she plowed her way through the water.

"I really should have been a skating princess," she said, lifting one leg straight up in the air so that the scrub brush on her left foot hit the ceiling lamp and broke off a piece.

"I've got grace and charm, at least," she went on, taking a big leap over a chair that stood in her way.

"Well, it must be clean by now," she said at last, and took off the brushes.

"Aren't you going to dry the floor?" asked Annika.

"Nope, it can dry in the sun," said Pippi. "I don't think it'll catch cold, as long as it keeps moving."

Tommy and Annika climbed down from the table and crossed the floor as carefully as they could so they wouldn't get wet.

Outside, the sun was shining in a bright blue sky. It was one of those dazzling September days when you feel like going for a walk in the woods. Pippi had an idea.

"What do you think about taking Mr. Nilsson with us and going on a little expedition?"

"Oh, yes," shouted Tommy and Annika with delight.

"Run home and ask your mother then," said Pippi.

"In the meantime I'll make a packed lunch."

Tommy and Annika thought that was a good plan. They dashed home, and it wasn't long before they were back. By then Pippi was already standing at the gate with Mr. Nilsson on her shoulder, a walking stick in one hand and a big basket in the other.

At first the children walked along the country road, but then they turned off into a field where a nice little path wound its way between birch trees and hazel thickets. After a while they came to a gate, and beyond the gate was a field that was even more beautiful. But a cow had taken up a position right in front of the gate, and she didn't look as if she wanted to move. Annika shouted at the cow, and Tommy bravely went over and tried to shove her aside, but she refused to budge from the spot. She just stared at the children with her big cow eyes. To put an end to the whole thing, Pippi set down the basket and went over and lifted the cow out of the way. Embarrassed, the cow lumbered off through the hazel thickets.

"To think that cows can be so bullheaded," said Pippi as she jumped over the gate, landing on both

feet. "And what happens then? Bulls get cowheaded, of course! It's really quite disgusting to think about."

"What a beautiful, beautiful field," cried Annika with delight, stepping from one rock to another. Tommy had brought along the dagger that Pippi had given him, and he cut walking sticks for both Annika and himself. He also cut his thumb a bit, but that didn't matter.

"Maybe we should pick a few toadstools," said Pippi, breaking off a beautiful red toadstool.

"I wonder if it's all right to eat this kind," she went on.

"You can't very well drink it, as far as I know,

so I suppose there's no other choice but to eat it.

I hope it's all right!"

95

She bit off a big piece of the toadstool and swallowed it.

"No problem," she proclaimed with delight. "Well, that's the kind we should collect and cook next time," she said, tossing the toadstool high over the treetops.

"What do you have in the basket, Pippi?" asked Annika. "Some goodies?"

"I'm not going to tell you, not even for a thousand kronor," Pippi told her. "First we have to find a good place where we can spread out everything."

The children eagerly began looking for just such a place. Annika found a big flat rock she thought was suitable, but it was swarming with red ants.

"I don't want to sit with them, because I haven't been properly introduced," said Pippi.

"And besides, they bite," said Tommy.

"Do they?" said Pippi. "Well, bite them back!"

Then Tommy caught sight of a small glade between a couple of hazel thickets, and that's where he thought they should sit.

"No, you know what? There's not enough sunshine

there to make my freckles happy," said Pippi. "And I think freckles are so nice-looking."

Some distance away was a small hill that could be easily and quickly climbed. On top of the hill was a sunny little ledge, just like a balcony. That's where they sat down.

"Now close your eyes while I take everything out," said Pippi. Tommy and Annika shut their eyes as tight as they could. They heard Pippi opening the basket and rustling some paper.

"One . . . two . . . nineteen . . . now you can look," Pippi said at last. And so they looked. And they shouted with delight when they saw all the treats that Pippi had set out on the bare rock. There were delicious little sandwiches with meatballs and ham, a whole stack of pancakes with sugar, several pieces of little brown sausage, and three pineapple puddings. Because you see, Pippi had learned all about preparing food from the cook on her father's ship.

"It's great having a house-cleaning holiday," said Tommy with his mouth full of pancake. "We should have them all the time."

"That's going too far," said Pippi. "I don't like cleaning that much. It's fun, there's no doubt about it, but not every day—that would get tiresome."

At last the children were so full that they could hardly move, and so they sat there in the sunshine, just enjoying themselves.

"I wonder whether it's hard to fly," said Pippi, peering over the rim of the ledge with a dreamy expression. There was a steep drop beneath them, and it was an awfully long way to the ground.

"It should be easy enough to learn to fly down," she went on. "I'm sure it's much harder to fly up. But a person could always start with the easiest part. I think I'll try it!"

"No, Pippi!" shouted both Tommy and Annika. "Oh, please, Pippi, don't do it!"

But Pippi was already standing on the edge of the precipice.

"Fly, you flighty flea, fly, and the flighty flea flew," she said, and as she said the word 'flew' she raised her arms and stepped off into thin air. Half a second later they heard a thud. That was Pippi hitting the ground.

Tommy and Annika lay down on their stomachs and peered down at her in terror.

Pippi stood up and brushed off her knees.

"I forgot to flap my arms," she said cheerfully. "Plus I probably have too many pancakes in my stomach."

At that moment the children realized that Mr. Nilsson had disappeared. He had apparently set off on a little expedition of his own. They remembered having seen him contentedly gnawing the lunch basket to shreds, but during Pippi's flying exercise they had forgotten all about him. And now he was gone.

Pippi got so angry that she threw one of her shoes into a big, deep pool of water.

"You should never take a monkey with you when you go anywhere," she said. "He *really* should have stayed at home and picked fleas off the horse. That would have served him right," she went on as she stepped into the pool to retrieve her shoe. The water came up to her waist.

"Actually, I might as well wash my hair while I'm here," said Pippi, ducking her head underwater for so long that bubbles started to surface.

"All right, now there's no need to go to the hairdresser this time," she continued, sounding pleased, when she finally reappeared. She climbed out of the water and put on her shoes. Then they set off to look for Mr. Nilsson.

"Hey, just listen to how it squishes when I walk!" laughed Pippi. "My clothes say 'squish, squish' and my shoes say 'slosh, slosh.' It's really funny. I think you should try it too," she said to Annika, who was walking along, looking so prim with her blonde silky hair, her pink dress, and her little white leather shoes.

"Some other time," said the sensible Annika.

They kept walking.

"It's easy to get mad at Mr. Nilsson," said Pippi. "He always does this. He once ran away from me in Surabaya and took a job as a servant with an old widow." After a pause she added, "That last part was a lie, of course."

Tommy suggested that they each go in a different direction to search. Annika was a little scared and at first didn't want to do it, but Tommy said, "You're not a coward, are you?"

That sort of scorn was too much for Annika. And so each of the three children went off in a different direction.

Tommy took the path across the meadow. He didn't find Mr. Nilsson, but he did find something else. A bull! Or rather, the bull found Tommy, and the bull didn't care for Tommy, because that bull was an angry animal and not at all fond of children. He came rushing over with his head lowered, bellowing horribly, and Tommy gave a loud yelp of terror that could be heard through the whole woods. Pippi and Annika heard it too and came running to see why Tommy was shouting like that. By then the bull had already managed to snag Tommy with his horns and had tossed him high up in the air.

"What a foolish bull that is," said Pippi to Annika, who was crying hard. "He shouldn't be doing things like that. He's getting Tommy's white sailor suit all dirty. I'm going to have to go and talk some sense into that stupid bull."

And she did. She ran over and tugged on his tail.
"Excuse me for breaking in," she said. Since she was
tugging quite hard, the bull turned
around and caught sight of another
child that he wanted to snag with his
horns. "As I said, excuse me
for breaking in,"
Pippi repeated.
"And excuse me
for breaking this
off," she added as she
broke off one of the
bull's horns. "This year it's
no longer fashionable to
have *two* horns," she
said. "This year all the
better bulls have only *one*
horn. Or none at all," she
said as she broke off the other
horn.

Since bulls have no feeling in
their horns, the bull didn't know

that his horns were gone. But he started vigorously butting Pippi, and if she had been anyone else, the bull would have made mincemeat of her.

"Ha ha ha, stop tickling me," cried Pippi. "You have no idea how ticklish I am. Ha ha, stop, stop, I'm going to die laughing!"

But the bull didn't stop, and finally Pippi jumped up onto his back to get a moment's peace. But the peace didn't last long, of course, because the bull didn't like having Pippi on his back. He started a terrific bucking to shake her off, but she just squeezed her legs tight and held on. The bull rushed back and forth in the meadow, bellowing so hard that smoke seemed to be pouring out of his nostrils. Pippi laughed and shrieked and waved to Tommy and Annika, who stood some distance away, shaking like aspen leaves. The bull spun around and around, trying to throw Pippi off.

"Here I am dancing with my little friend," hummed Pippi, not budging from where she sat. Finally the bull was so tired that he lay down on the ground, wishing that there were no children in the whole

wide world. For that matter, he never had thought that children were especially necessary.

"Are you planning to take an afternoon nap now?" Pippi asked the bull politely. "In that case, I won't disturb you."

She climbed down from his back and went over to Tommy and Annika. Tommy had been crying a little. He had a cut on one arm, but Annika had wrapped her handkerchief around it, and it didn't hurt anymore.

"Oh, Pippi," shouted Annika, bubbling with excitement, when Pippi came over to them.

"Shh," whispered Pippi. "Don't wake the bull! He's sleeping, and if we wake him up he'll just get cranky."

But the next second she shouted in a loud voice, "Mr. Nilsson, Mr. Nilsson, where are you?" She wasn't paying any attention to the bull's afternoon nap. "We have to go home now."

And believe it or not, there sat Mr. Nilsson, huddled up in a pine tree. He was sucking on his tail and looked quite miserable. It was no fun for such a little monkey to be left all alone in the woods. Now he scampered down from the pine tree and leaped onto Pippi's shoulder. He began waving his straw hat the way he always did whenever he was really happy.

"So, you didn't become a servant this time, did you?" said Pippi, stroking his back. "No wait, that's true, it was a lie," she added. "But if it was true, it couldn't be a lie, could it?" she pondered. "When all is said and done, he might actually have been a servant in Surabaya, after all! If so, I know who's going to make the meatballs from now on."

And then they headed home. Pippi's

dress was still squishing, and her shoes were sloshing. Tommy and Annika thought they'd had a wonderful day in spite of the bull, and they sang a song that they'd learned in school. It was actually a summer song, but even though it would soon be autumn, they thought that it was the right song to be singing:

On a summery and sunny day
we walk through green woods on the way,
not a word of complaint, come what may.
We sing as we go. **Sing high, sing low!**
The young among you
come and sing too.
Don't sit home with nothing to do.
Our singing group
climbs as one troop,
reaching the top in one fell swoop.
On a summery and sunny day
we sing as we go. **Sing high, sing low!**

Pippi sang along too, but she wasn't really singing the same words. This is what she sang:

On a summery and sunny day
I walk through green woods on the way,
saying whatever I want to say.

And it sloshes as I go.
SLOSH slow, SLOSH slow!
And in my shoe
it squishes too.

It says first AHEM and then ah-choo.
My shoe is wet.
A bull we met.

Rice pudding is the best thing yet.
On a summery and sunny day
it sloshes as I go.

SLOSH slow, SLOSH slow!

Chapter Seven

Pippi Goes to the Circus

A circus had come to the little town, and all the children ran to their mothers and fathers to ask permission to go. Tommy and Annika did too, and their nice pappa promptly gave them several lovely silver kronor. With the coins held tightly in their hands, they rushed off to find Pippi. She was on the porch with her horse,

busy twisting his tail into tiny braids, which she tied with red bows.

"It's his birthday today. At least I think it is," she said. "And that's why he has to look nice."

"Pippi," said Tommy, huffing and puffing because they had run so fast, "Pippi, do you want to go to the circus?"

"I can go to almost anything," said Pippi, "but I'm not sure whether I can go to a surkus because I don't know what a surkus is. Does it hurt?"

"Don't be silly," said Tommy. "Of course it doesn't hurt! It's lots of fun! With horses and clowns and beautiful ladies walking on tightropes!"

"But it costs money," said Annika, and she opened her little hand to see if the coins were still there—a big shiny two-krona coin and two fifty-öre coins.

"I'm as rich as a troll," said Pippi. "So I can always buy myself a surkus. Although it might get a bit crowded if I'm going to have more horses. I can always stack up the clowns and those beautiful ladies in the laundry room, but it's going to be harder to find room for the horses."

"Silly," said Tommy. "You're not supposed to buy the circus. Don't you understand? It costs money to go in and look."

"Good gracious," cried Pippi, shutting her eyes. "It costs money to look? And here I go around staring all day long! Who knows how much money I've already spent on my staring!"

After a while, she cautiously opened one eye and rolled it around. "I don't care what it costs," she said, "I just have to have a look!"

Finally Tommy and Annika managed to explain to Pippi what a circus was. Then Pippi went to get several gold coins from her suitcase. After that she put on her hat, which was as big as a mill wheel, and then they hurried off to the circus.

A big crowd had gathered outside the circus tent, and there was a long line at the ticket window. Eventually it was Pippi's turn. She stuck her head inside the window, stared hard at the nice old lady who was sitting there, and said, "So how much does it cost to look at you?"

But the old lady was a foreigner, and she didn't understand what Pippi meant, so she said: "Little girl, it costs fife kronor for front zeats and three kronor for zeats in the back and one krona for schtanding room."

"All right," said Pippi. "But then you have to promise to walk the tightrope too."

Now Tommy stepped forward and said that Pippi wanted a seat in the back. Pippi handed over a gold coin, and the old lady gave it a suspicious look. She even bit it to make sure it was real. Finally she was convinced that the coin was made of real gold, and she handed Pippi a ticket. She also gave her a lot of silver coins in change.

"What am I supposed to do with all these horrid little white coins?" said Pippi annoyed. "Why don't you just keep them. Then I can look at you twice instead of just once. From the schtanding room."

Since Pippi absolutely refused to accept any change, the woman gave her a ticket for a front-row seat instead. She also gave Tommy and Annika front-row tickets, and they didn't even have to spend any of their own money. That was how Pippi and Tommy and Annika ended up sitting on fancy red chairs right next to the circus ring. Tommy and Annika kept turning around to wave to their classmates who were sitting much farther back.

"What a strange tent this is," said Pippi, looking around in surprise. "And I see that they've spilled sawdust on the floor. Not that I'm fussy about such things, but I do think it looks rather messy."

Tommy explained to Pippi that every circus had sawdust on the floor. It was for the horses to run on.

Up on a platform sat the circus band, which suddenly began playing a thundering march. Pippi clapped her hands wildly and jumped up and down in her chair with delight.

"Does it also cost something to listen, or can we do that for free?" she asked.

At that moment a curtain was pulled aside from the performers' entrance, and the ringmaster, wearing a black coat and with a whip in his hand, came running in. Behind him came ten white horses with red plumes on their heads.

The ringmaster cracked his whip, and the horses galloped around the ring.

Then the ringmaster cracked his whip again and all the horses stood on their hind legs with their front hooves up on the low wall surrounding the ring. One of the horses came to a halt right in front of where the children were sitting. Annika didn't like having a horse so close, and she shrank as far back in her seat as she could.

But Pippi leaned forward, lifted up the horse's front hoof and said, "Glad to meet you! I bring you many greetings from my *own* horse. He has a birthday today, just like you, but he has bows on his tail instead of on his head."

Luckily Pippi let go of the horse's hoof before the ringmaster cracked his whip again, because then all the horses hopped down from the low wall and went back to galloping.

When the performance was over, the ringmaster bowed politely and the horses trotted off through the exit. The next moment the curtain opened once again for a black horse, and on his back stood a beautiful lady wearing green silk tights. It said in the program that her name was Señorita Carmencita.

The horse trotted around in the sawdust, and Señorita Carmencita stood calmly on his back, smiling. But then something happened. Just as the horse passed the spot where Pippi was sitting, something whooshed through the air—and that something was none other than Pippi. And there she stood on the horse's back behind Señorita Carmencita. At first Señorita Carmencita was so surprised that she almost fell off the horse. Then she got really angry. She started flailing her hands behind her to make Pippi jump off. But it did no good.

"Calm down a couple of notches," said Pippi. "Surely you're not the only one who's allowed to have any fun. Other people have paid for a ticket too—I'm sure of that!"

Then Señorita Carmencita tried to jump off the horse, but again without success because Pippi had a firm grip around her waist.

And then all the spectators at the circus couldn't help laughing. They thought it looked so ridiculous to see the beautiful Señorita Carmencita held tight by a little red-headed girl who stood there on the horse's back with her big shoes, looking as if performing in a circus was the most natural thing in the world for her.

But the ringmaster wasn't laughing. He gave a signal to his red-coated attendants to rush forward and stop the horse.

"Is the show already over?" said Pippi, disappointed. "Just when we were having so much fun!"

"You schtupid child," snarled the ringmaster through clenched teeth. "Get out!"

Pippi gave him a distressed look.

"What's going on?" she said. "Why are you so mad at me? I thought we were supposed to be having a good time."

She jumped off the horse and went back to her seat. But then two big attendants came over to throw her out. They grabbed hold of Pippi and tried to lift her.

But they couldn't do it. Pippi sat absolutely still, and there was no way they could budge her from the spot, no matter how hard they tried. So they shrugged their shoulders and left.

In the meantime, the next act had started. It was Miss Elvira, who was going to walk the tightrope. She wore a pink tulle dress, and she had a pink parasol in her hand. Taking dainty little steps, she ran along the tightrope. She swung her legs and did all sorts of acrobatics. It looked so sweet. She even showed that she could walk backward on the slender rope. But when she came back to the small platform at one end of the tightrope and turned around, there stood Pippi.

"Quite a surprise, isn't it?" said Pippi with delight when she saw Miss Elvira's astonished expression.

Miss Elvira didn't say a word. Instead she jumped down from the tightrope and threw her arms around the neck of the ringmaster, who happened to be her father. And the ringmaster once again sent his attendants to throw Pippi out. This time he sent five of them.

But then all the spectators in the circus started shouting, "Leave her alone! We want to see the red-headed girl!"

And they all stamped their feet and clapped their hands.

Pippi leaped onto the tightrope. And Miss Elvira's acrobatics were nothing

compared to what Pippi could do.

When she reached the middle of the tightrope, she stretched one leg high in the air, and her big shoe spread out like a roof over her head. She bent her foot forward slightly so that she could tickle herself behind one ear.

The ringmaster was not at all pleased with Pippi performing in his circus. He wanted to get rid of her. That's why he sneaked over to release the mechanism that held the rope tight. He was sure that Pippi would come tumbling down.

But she didn't. Instead Pippi started the rope swaying. Back and forth swung the rope. Pippi swayed faster and faster, and then—all of a sudden—she stepped out into the air and landed right on the ringmaster's back. He was so startled that he began to run.

"What a fun horse you are," said Pippi. "But why don't you have any tassels in your hair?"

Now Pippi thought it was time to go back to Tommy and Annika. She climbed off the ringmaster's back and returned to her seat, just as the next act was about to start. There was a slight delay because the ringmaster first had to go out and drink a glass of water and comb his hair.

But then he came back in, bowed to the audience, and said, "Ladies and chentlemen! In a moment you vill behold the greatest marfel of our time, the schtrongest man in the world. Schtrong Adolf, who iss schtill undefeated. And now, ladies and chentlemen, I give you Schtrong Adolf!"

And into the ring stepped a giant of a man. He was dressed in flesh-colored tights, with a leopard skin wrapped around his waist. He bowed to the audience, looking very pleased with himself.

"Chust look at these muschles," said the ring-master as he squeezed Strong Adolf's arm where the muscles bulged like bowling balls under his skin.

"And now, ladies and chentlemen, now I haff a truly grand offer to make! Who among you vill dare attempt a wrestling match with Schtrong Adolf? Who vill dare defeat the world's schtrongest man? I'll pay a hundert kronor to whosoever can defeat Schtrong Adolf. One hundert kronor—keep that in mind, ladies and chentlemen! All right! Who vill schtep forvard?"

No one
stepped forward.
"What did he say?" asked Pippi.
"And why is he speaking Arabic?"
"He said that whoever can beat that
huge man will get a hundred kronor,"
said Tommy.
"I could do that," said Pippi. "But I
think it would be a shame to beat
him, because he looks
so nice."

124

"Oh, but I'm sure you couldn't do it anyway," said Annika. "He's the world's strongest man, after all!"

"*Man*, yes," said Pippi. "But I'm the world's strongest *girl*—keep that in mind!"

In the meantime Strong Adolf was lifting huge iron weights and bending thick iron bars in half to show how strong he was.

125

"Zo, ladies and chentlemen," shouted the ring-master, "iss there rrreally no one who vishes to earn a hundert kronor? Am I rrreally going to haff to keep the money all for myself?" he said, waving a hundred-krona note in the air.

"No, I **rrreally** don't think so," said Pippi, and she climbed over the low wall and into the ring.

The ringmaster flew into a rage when he caught sight of her.

"Get out, get lost, I don't vant to see you," he snarled.

"Why do you always have to be so unfriendly?" said Pippi reproachfully. "All I want to do is fight with Strong Adolf."

"This iss no place for jokes," said the ringmaster. "Get out of here before Schtrong Adolf hears how schameless you are!"

But Pippi walked right past the ringmaster and over to Strong Adolf. She grabbed his big hand and gave it a hearty shake.

"All right, shall we have a little tussle, you and I?" she said.

Strong Adolf looked at her, uncomprehending.

"In one minute I'm going to start," said Pippi.

And she did. She took a firm grip on Strong Adolf's waist, and before anyone knew what had happened, she had him down on the mat. Strong Adolf leaped to his feet, his face bright red.

"Hooray for Pippi!" shouted Tommy and Annika.

All the spectators in the circus heard them, and then they too shouted, "Hooray for Pippi!"

The ringmaster was sitting on the low wall and wringing his hands. He was angry.

But Strong Adolf was even angrier. Never in his life had he experienced anything so awful. Now he was certainly going to have to show this red-headed girl what sort of man Strong Adolf really was. He rushed at her and grabbed her around the waist. But Pippi stood there as steady as a rock.

"You can do better than that," she said, trying to encourage him. But then she pried herself loose from his grip, and in an instant Strong Adolf was once again lying on the mat. Pippi stood next to him, waiting. And she didn't have long to wait. With a howl he got to his feet and again came storming towards her.

"**Tiddly-pom** and **piddly-dee**," said Pippi.

All the spectators at the circus stamped their feet, tossed their caps in the air, and shouted, "Hooray for Pippi!"

When Strong Adolf came rushing at her for the third time, Pippi lifted him high in the air and, holding her arms straight up, she carried him around the ring. Then she put him back down on the mat and held him there.

"All right, my dear man, I think we've had enough of this for now," she said. "It's not going to get any more fun than this, that's for sure."

"Pippi is the winner, Pippi is the winner," shouted all the spectators at the circus. Strong Adolf slunk away as fast as he could. And the ringmaster was forced to go over and hand Pippi the hundred-krona note, even though he looked as if he would rather swallow her whole.

"Here you are, my dear," he said. "Here you are, one hundert kronor."

"What's this?" said Pippi scornfully. "What am I supposed to do with this piece of paper? Go ahead and fry herring in it if you like!"

And she went back to her seat.

"This is a very long surkus," she said to Tommy and Annika. "I wouldn't mind a little catnap. But wake me up if you need my help with anything else."

And then she leaned back in her seat and instantly fell asleep. And there she lay, snoring, as the clowns and sword-swallowers and contortionists performed their tricks for Tommy and Annika and all the other spectators at the circus.

"But I really think Pippi was the best of all," Tommy whispered to Annika.

Chapter Eight

Pippi Dances with Burglars

After Pippi's performance at the circus, there wasn't a single person in the whole little town who didn't know how incredibly strong she was. There was even something about her in the newspaper. But people who lived elsewhere, of course, didn't know who Pippi was.

One dark autumn night two tramps came trudging along the road past Villa Villekulla. The tramps were two shabby burglars who had set off to roam through the country, looking for things to steal. They saw lights on in the windows of Villa Villekulla, and they decided to go inside and ask for a sandwich.

That night Pippi had poured all her gold coins out on the kitchen floor, and she was sitting there counting them. She wasn't actually very good at counting, but occasionally she did it all the same. Just to keep things in order.

". . . seventy-five, seventy-six, seventy-seven, seventy-eight, seventy-nine, seventy-ten, seventy-eleven, seventy-twelve, seventy-thirteen, seventy-seventeen . . . I seem to be stuck on seventy! Good gracious, surely there must be some other numbers in the number nebula. Oh, that's right, I remember now: one hundred and four, one thousand. That's certainly a lot of money," said Pippi.

At that moment someone pounded on the door.

"Come in or stay outside, whatever you like," yelled Pippi. "I'm not forcing anybody!"

The door opened and the two tramps came in. Just imagine how big their eyes got when they saw a little red-headed girl sitting on the floor all alone, counting money!

"Are you home by yourself?" they asked slyly.

"Not at all," said Pippi. "Mr. Nilsson is home too."

The burglars couldn't know, of course, that Mr. Nilsson was a little monkey who was asleep in his green-painted bed with a doll's blanket pulled over him. They thought that the master of the house was named Nilsson, and they gave each other a meaningful wink.

"Let's come back a little later," was what they meant by that wink. But to Pippi they said, "Well, we just came in to see what your clock says."

They were so excited that they forgot all about the sandwiches.

"Big, strong fellows like you, and you don't even know what a clock says?" said Pippi. "Who brought you up, anyway? Haven't you ever heard a clock before? A clock is a little round **thingamajig** that says 'tick tock' and keeps going and going but never gets to the door. If you know any other riddles, let's hear them," said Pippi to encourage them.

The tramps thought that Pippi was too young to know about clocks, so without another word they turned on their heels and left.

"I'm not asking you to play tic-tac-toe!" Pippi

yelled after them. "But you could at least play along with my tick-tock riddle. I don't know what makes you tick! But never mind, go in peace," said Pippi, and she went back to counting her money.

Safely outside, the tramps rubbed their hands with glee.

"Did you see all that money? Good heavens!" said one of them.

"Yeah, we're really in luck," said the other. "All we have to do is wait until the girl and that Nilsson go to sleep. Then we'll sneak inside and get our mitts on all that money."

They sat down under an oak tree in the garden to wait. It was drizzling, and they were very hungry, so it wasn't especially pleasant, but the thought of all that money kept their spirits high.

The lights went out in the other houses, one by one, but in Villa Villekulla the lights stayed on. This was because Pippi was learning to dance a polka, and she didn't want to go to bed until she was positive that she could do it right. But finally the windows in Villa Villekulla also went dark.

The tramps waited quite a while to make sure that Mr. Nilsson would be asleep. Finally they sneaked over to the kitchen door and got ready to pry it open with their burglary tools. Then one of them—whose name was Blom, by the way—happened by chance to try the door. It wasn't locked.

"How stupid can people be?" he whispered to his partner. "Look at this—the door is open!"

"All the better for us," replied his partner, a black-haired man called Thunder-Karlsson by those who knew him.

Thunder-Karlsson switched on his flashlight, and then they sneaked into the kitchen. No one was there. The room next to it was Pippi's bedroom, which was also where Mr. Nilsson's little doll's bed stood.

Thunder-Karlsson opened the door

and cautiously

p e e k e d   inside.

It   was   nice

and   quiet,

and he let the beam of his flashlight play

over the room.

When the beam came to Pippi's bed, both tramps saw to their surprise that there was nothing but a pair of feet resting on the pillow. As usual, Pippi had her head under the covers at the foot of the bed.

"That must be the girl," whispered Thunder-Karlsson to Blom. "And she seems to be sound asleep. But where on earth do you think Nilsson is?"

"*Mister* Nilsson, if you don't mind," said Pippi's calm voice from under the covers. "*Mister* Nilsson is sleeping in the little green doll's bed."

The tramps were so startled that they were just about to rush out. But then they happened to think about what Pippi had said. Mr. Nilsson was sleeping in the doll's bed. And in the beam of the flashlight they caught sight of the doll's bed and the little monkey who was lying in it. Thunder-Karlsson couldn't help laughing.

"Blom," he said. "Mr. Nilsson is a monkey, ha ha ha!"

"Well, what did you think he was?" said Pippi's calm voice from under the covers. "A lawnmower?"

"Aren't your mamma and pappa home?" asked Blom.

"Nope," said Pippi. "They're gone! Gone far away!"

Thunder-Karlsson and Blom were so delighted that they started chuckling.

"Now listen here, little girl," said Thunder-Karlsson, "come out of there so we can talk to you!"

"Nope," said Pippi. "I'm sleeping. Does this have to do with more riddles? If that's the case, you'll have to answer this one first: What kind of clock goes and goes but never gets to the door?"

Then Blom took a firm grip on the covers and lifted them off.

"Can you dance a polka?" asked Pippi, giving him a serious look. "I can!"

"You ask too many questions," said Thunder-Karlsson. "Why don't you let us ask a few questions now? For instance, where did you put the money that you had out on the floor a while ago?"

"In the suitcase in the cabinet," replied Pippi truthfully.

Thunder-Karlsson and Blom grinned.

"I hope you won't mind, my dear, if we take it," said Thunder-Karlsson.

"Oh, not at all," said Pippi. "Of course not."

And with that, Blom went over and took out the suitcase.

"I hope you won't mind, my dear, if I take it back," said Pippi, as she climbed out of bed and went over to Blom.

Blom didn't really know what happened, but somehow the suitcase suddenly ended up in Pippi's hand.

"Quit joking around," said Thunder-Karlsson angrily. "Give me that suitcase!"

He grabbed Pippi hard by the arm and tried to yank the plunder away from her.

"Who says I was joking?" said Pippi as she lifted

Thunder-Karlsson on top of the cabinet. The next instant Blom was sitting there too. Then both of the tramps were scared. They began to realize that Pippi was not exactly an ordinary girl. But the suitcase was still tempting them, so they pushed aside their fear.

"All together now, Blom," shouted Thunder-Karlsson, and then they jumped down from the cabinet and rushed at Pippi, who was holding the suitcase in her hand. But Pippi jabbed them with her finger and they each landed in opposite corners of the room. Before they could get to their feet, Pippi got out a rope, and quick as a wink she tied up the arms and legs of both burglars. Now they started singing a different tune.

"My dear, sweet little girl," pleaded Thunder-Karlsson. "Please forgive us. We were only joking! Don't hurt us. We're just a couple of poor tramps who came in to ask for a little food."

Blom even managed to shed a few tears.

Pippi put the suitcase back in its place in the cabinet. Then she turned to face her prisoners.

"Can either of you dance a polka?"

"Hmm . . . well . . ." said Thunder-Karlsson. "I suppose we both can."

"Oh, what fun!" said Pippi, clapping her hands. "Couldn't we dance for a bit? I've just learned how, you see."

"Er . . . of course," said Thunder-Karlsson, rather surprised.

Then Pippi got out a big pair of scissors and cut off the ropes that were holding her visitors.

"But we don't have any music," said Pippi anxiously. Then she had an idea.

"Could you blow on a comb?" she said to Blom. "Then I'll dance with him." And she pointed to Thunder-Karlsson.

Yes, of course, Blom could blow on a comb. And that's what he did, so loudly that it could be heard through the whole house. Mr. Nilsson was startled awake, and he sat up in bed just in time to see Pippi whirling around with Thunder-Karlsson. Her expression was dead serious, and she was dancing with such energy, as if her life depended on it.

Finally Blom refused to blow on the comb any more because he claimed that it was tickling his lips so terribly. And Thunder-Karlsson's legs were starting to get tired, since he'd been trudging along the road all day long.

"Oh please, just a little bit more," begged Pippi as she kept on dancing. And there was nothing for Blom and Thunder-Karlsson to do but keep going.

When it was three in the morning, Pippi said, "Oh, I could keep on like this until Thursday! But maybe you're tired or hungry?"

That was exactly what they were, although they hardly dared say so. From the pantry Pippi brought out bread and cheese and butter and ham and a cold roast and milk, and then they all sat down at the table—Blom and Thunder-Karlsson and Pippi—and they ate until they were stuffed to the gills.

Pippi poured a little milk in one ear. "It's good for an earache," she said.

"You poor thing. Do you have an earache?" asked Blom.

"Nope," said Pippi. "But I might get one."

Finally both tramps stood up, thanked Pippi for the food, and said that they would have to be going.

"I'm *so* glad you came! Do you *really* have to leave so soon?" said Pippi sadly. "I've never seen anyone who can dance a polka like you can, my sweet little sugar pig," she said to Thunder-Karlsson. "And be sure to keep practicing at playing the comb," she told Blom. "Then you won't notice that it tickles."

As they headed out of the door Pippi came running to give each of them a gold coin.

"You've certainly earned it," she said.

Chapter Nine

Pippi Has Coffee with the Ladies

Tommy and Annika's mother had invited several ladies over for coffee, and since she had done so much baking, she said that Tommy and Annika could invite Pippi at the same time. That way her own children would be much less trouble, or so she believed.

Tommy and Annika were thrilled when they heard this, and they immediately ran over to Pippi's house to invite her. Pippi was in her garden using an old rusty watering can to water whatever poor flowers were still left. Since rain was pouring down from the sky that day, Tommy told Pippi that it didn't really seem necessary.

"Well, that's easy for you to say," said Pippi sternly. "But I lay awake all night, looking forward to getting up and watering my flowers, so I'm not going to let a little rain stop me, let me tell you!"

Then Annika told her the wonderful news.

"Coffee with the ladies . . . *me*?" cried Pippi. And she got so nervous that she started to water Tommy instead of the rosebush as she had intended. "Oh, I don't know! It makes me nervous. What if I can't behave properly?"

"I'm sure you can," said Annika.

"Don't be so sure about that," said Pippi. "I'll do my best, believe me. But I've noticed many times that people don't think I can behave properly, even though I try my very best. Out at sea we were never so fussy about such things. But I promise to try really hard today so that you won't have to be ashamed of me."

"Good," said Tommy, and then he and Annika raced back home through the rain.

"This afternoon at three o'clock. Don't forget," called Annika, peeking out from under her umbrella.

That afternoon at

three o'clock

a very elegant young lady

went up the stairs

to the Settergren home.

It was Pippi Longstocking. For a change she was not wearing her red hair in braids. It hung down to her shoulders like a lion's mane. She had used a red crayon to color her lips bright red, and she had made her eyebrows so dark that she looked slightly sinister. She had also used the red crayon to color her fingernails, and on her shoes she wore big green bows.

"I know I'm going to be the most elegant person at this party," she muttered happily to herself as she rang the doorbell.

In the Settergrens' living room sat three refined ladies, along with Tommy and Annika and their mother. A marvelous spread of food had been set on the table, and a fire was burning in the fireplace. The ladies were quietly chatting with each other as Tommy and Annika sat on the sofa and looked through a photo album. Everything was so peaceful.

But suddenly the peace was shattered.

"Company—ATTEN-SHUN!"

A piercing shout came from the hall, and the next second Pippi Longstocking was standing in the doorway. She had shouted so loudly and so unexpectedly that the ladies had actually jumped.

"Company—forward, MARCH!" Pippi shouted next, and then she marched briskly over to Mrs. Settergren.

"Company—HALT!" She stopped.

"Present arms, one, TWO!" she yelled, and she used both hands to grab one of Mrs. Settergren's, which she shook quite heartily.

"Knees, BEND!" she shouted, and she curtsied beautifully.

Then she smiled at Mrs. Settergren and said in her usual voice, "I'm actually quite shy, so if I didn't issue commands to myself I'd just stand in the hall, quite stubborn, and not dare to come in."

After that she rushed over to the other ladies and kissed each of them on the cheek.

"Charmed, charmed, I'm sure," she said because she had once heard a distinguished gentleman say this to a lady. And then she sat down on the best chair in the room. Mrs. Settergren had planned for the children to stay upstairs in Tommy and Annika's room, but Pippi calmly sat where she was, slapping her knees and casting glances at the food on the table.

"That looks delicious. When do we start?"

At that instant, Ella, the family's maid, came in with the coffeepot. Mrs. Settergren said, "Coffee is served!"

"Me first," shouted Pippi, and with two bounds she was over at the table. She piled onto a plate as many little cakes as it would hold, tossed five lumps of sugar into a coffee cup, emptied half the cream jug into her cup, and then went back to her chair with her plunder before the ladies had even reached the table.

Pippi stretched out her legs and balanced the plate of cakes between the tips of her toes. Then she swiftly started dipping cakes in her coffee. She stuffed so many of them in her mouth at once that she couldn't have uttered a word, no matter how hard she tried.

In the blink of an eye she finished off all the cakes on her plate. She got up, slapped the plate like a tambourine, and went back to the table to see if there were any more cakes left. The ladies gave her a disapproving look, but she didn't take any notice. Cheerfully chattering, she walked around the table, snatching a cake here and a cake there.

"It was awfully nice of you to invite me," she said. "I've never been invited to coffee before."

There was a big cream cake on the table. In the middle of it was a piece of red candy as a decoration. Pippi stood with her hands behind her back and looked at it. All of a sudden she leaned forward and snatched up the candy in her teeth. But she had bent down a little too quickly, and when she straightened up, her whole face was covered with cream.

"Ha ha ha," laughed Pippi. "Now we can play

blindman's-buff, because we already have a blindfold, and it's absolutely free. I can't see a thing."

Then she stuck out her tongue and licked off all the cream.

"Well, that was really quite an accident," she said. "But now the cake is just going to go to waste, so I might as well eat the whole thing."

And she did. She launched into it with a cake server, and in a matter of minutes the whole cake was gone. Pippi patted her stomach contentedly. Mrs. Settergren had gone out to the kitchen for a moment so she knew nothing about the accident with the cake. But the other ladies were giving Pippi very stern looks. They probably would have liked some of that cake themselves. Pippi noticed that they didn't look pleased, and she decided to cheer them up.

"Let's not be sad about such a small and unfortunate incident," she consoled them. "The main thing is that we have our health. And besides, you're supposed to have fun when you're invited for coffee."

She picked up the sugar bowl and scattered the lumps of sugar all over the floor.

"Oh, what's this?" she cried in a shrill voice. "How could I ever make such a *mistake*! I thought it was granulated sugar, the kind that you're supposed to sprinkle. But now the damage is done. Luckily there's only one thing to do if you happen to sprinkle lumps of sugar by mistake—you have to do the opposite and try to make the granulated sugar into lumps."

With these words she picked up a container of granulated sugar from the table and sprinkled sugar on her tongue, trying hard to shape it into lumps.

"Well, there you see," she said. "If it doesn't work, nothing will."

Then she took the container of granulated sugar and sprinkled a large amount onto the floor.

"Please note, this is *granulated* sugar," she said. "So I'm perfectly entitled to do this. Because I'd like to know what good it is to have granulated sugar if you can't use it for sprinkling.

"Have you ever noticed how much fun it is to walk on sugar that's been spilled on the floor?" she asked the ladies. "It's even more fun it you're barefoot," she went on, tearing off her shoes and stockings. "You really should try it yourselves. Nothing feels better. You can take my word for it."

Now Mrs. Settergren came back in from the kitchen. When she saw all the spilled sugar, she grabbed Pippi hard by the arm and led her over to Tommy and Annika, who were sitting on the sofa. Then she went to sit with the ladies, offering them more coffee. The fact that the cake was gone made her happy. She thought that her guests had liked it so much that they had eaten the whole thing.

Pippi, Tommy, and Annika were talking quietly over on the sofa. The fire was crackling in the fireplace. The ladies were having another cup of coffee, and everything was once again nice and peaceful. Then, as sometimes happens when ladies gather for coffee, they started talking about their maids. They didn't seem to have found very good maids, because they weren't the least bit happy with them. They agreed that they really shouldn't have maids at all. It would actually be much better to do everything themselves, because then at least they would know that it was done properly.

Pippi sat on the sofa, listening, and when the ladies had gone on like this for a while, she said, "My grandmother once had a maid whose name was Malin. She had chilblains on her feet, but otherwise there was nothing wrong with her. The only annoying thing was that as soon as any visitors turned up, she would dash over to them and bite them on the leg. And bark! Oh, how she would bark! You could hear it all over the neighborhood. She was just being playful, but the visitors didn't always understand that. The old wife of a vicar once came to visit Grandma just after Malin had started working there. When Malin came running over and sank her teeth into the old woman's shin, the vicar's wife gave a howl. It scared Malin so badly that she sank her teeth in even deeper. And then she couldn't get loose. She was stuck like that, on the leg of the vicar's wife, until Friday. So Grandma had to peel the potatoes herself that day. But at least it was properly done. She peeled them so well that when she was finished, there were no potatoes left at all. Only peels! After that Friday the vicar's wife never came to see Grandma again. She

really had no sense of humor. And Malin was just being playful and merry! But it can't be denied that once in a while she could also be rather moody. Once when Grandma stuck a fork in Malin's ear, she spent the whole day sulking."

Pippi gave everyone a friendly smile.

"Well, that was Malin. Yes, it was," she said as she twiddled her thumbs.

The ladies pretended they hadn't heard a word. They kept on chatting.

"If only my Rosa were at least clean and tidy," said Mrs. Berggren, "then I might be able to keep her on. But she's like a pig."

"Then you should have seen Malin," Pippi piped up. "Grandma said that Malin was so grubby and grimy that it was a sight to behold. For a long time Grandma thought that she actually had dark skin, but it was all just dirt that could be washed right off. One time at a bazaar at the City Hotel, she won first prize for the amount of black grime under her fingernails. Oh yes, goodness gracious, how filthy that girl was," said Pippi merrily.

Mrs. Settergren gave her a stern look.

"Can you believe it?" said Mrs. Granberg. "The other evening, when my Britta was going out, she borrowed my blue silk dress without even asking. Isn't that the height of impudence?"

"It certainly is," said Pippi. "I can hear that she and Malin are two of a kind. Grandma had a pink camisole, and she was terribly fond of it. But the worst thing was that Malin was fond of it too. And every morning Grandma and Malin would fight over who was going to wear that camisole. They finally agreed that they would take turns, in order to be fair. But just think how mean Malin could be! Sometimes she would come running in when it wasn't even her turn and say: 'There won't be any mashed turnips if I don't get to wear that pink woolen camisole!' Well, what was Grandma to do? Mashed turnips were her favorite dish. There was nothing to be done but give Malin that camisole! And once she got it, she would go out to the kitchen, as nice as you please, and start mashing turnips so hard that they splattered all over the walls."

For a moment no one spoke.

Then Mrs. Alexandersson said, "I'm not absolutely certain about this, but I have a strong suspicion that my Hulda is stealing. I do know that I've noticed things have been missing."

"Malin . . ." Pippi began.

But then Mrs. Settergren said firmly, "Children, go up to your room. Right now!"

"Yes, but I was just going to tell you that Malin stole things too," said Pippi. "Just like a magpie! Anything that wasn't nailed down! She used to get up in the middle of the night to steal a few things, because she said that otherwise she couldn't sleep peacefully. Once she swiped Grandma's piano and stuffed it in the top drawer of her own dresser. Grandma said that she had very nimble fingers."

Now Tommy and Annika took Pippi by the arms and started pulling her up the stairs. The ladies were drinking their third cup of coffee, and Mrs. Settergren said, "It's not that I really want to complain about my Ella, but she certainly does break a lot of china."

A red head came into view over the banister.

"Speaking of Malin," said Pippi, "maybe you were wondering whether she used to break any china. Well, you could certainly say that again! She set aside a specific day of the week for breaking china. Grandma told me that it was on Tuesdays. By five in the morning on Tuesday you could already hear that splendid girl smashing china out in the kitchen. She started with the coffee cups and glasses and other smaller items, moved on to the soup plates and then the dinner plates, and ended with the meat platters and soup tureens. Grandma said she was happy to hear such a crashing in the kitchen all morning long. And if Malin had any time left over later in the afternoon, she would go into the sitting room with a little hammer and smash the antique East Indian plates that hung on the walls. Grandma always bought new china on Wednesdays," said Pippi, and she vanished up the stairs like a jack-in-the-box.

By now Mrs. Settergren's patience had come to an end. She ran up the stairs, into the children's room, and over to Pippi, who had just started to teach Tommy how to stand on his head.

"You're not allowed to come here again," said Mrs. Settergren, "not when you behave so badly."

Pippi looked at her in surprise, and slowly her eyes filled with tears. "It's just like I thought," she said. "I knew I wouldn't be able to behave myself! It's not even worth trying—I'm never going to learn how anyway. I should have stayed at sea."

Then she curtsied to Mrs. Settergren, said good-bye to Tommy and Annika, and slowly went downstairs.

But now it was also time for the ladies to go home. Pippi sat down on the boot rack in the hall and watched as they put on their coats and hats.

"It's a shame that you don't like your maids," she said. "You should have someone like Malin! Grandma always said that you couldn't find a more wonderful maid. Just think, one Christmas when Malin was supposed to serve a roast pig—do you know what she did? She had read in the cookbook that a Christmas pig should be served with paper frills on the ears and an apple in the mouth. And poor Malin didn't realize that it was the pig that was supposed to have the apple. You should have seen her when she came in on Christmas Eve, wearing her starched apron and with a big apple in her mouth. Grandma said to her, 'What a fool you are, Malin!' And of course Malin couldn't utter a word in her own defense. All she could do was wiggle her ears so the paper frills rustled. She did try to say something, but it just came out as '**Blub, blub, blub**.' And she couldn't bite anyone on the leg, the way she usually did, even though there were so many visitors present that day. No, it wasn't a very pleasant Christmas Eve for poor little Malin," said Pippi sadly.

The ladies now had their coats on, and they were saying a last good-bye to Mrs. Settergren.

Pippi ran over to her and whispered, "I'm sorry that I couldn't behave myself! Good-bye!"

Then she slapped her big hat on her head and followed the ladies out the door. But outside the gate they went their separate ways. Pippi headed for Villa Villekulla, and the ladies headed in the opposite direction.

After they had walked a short distance, they heard someone huffing and puffing behind them. It was Pippi, who had come dashing after them.

"Believe me, Grandma was sad when she lost Malin. Just think, one Tuesday morning when Malin hadn't even managed to smash more than a dozen teacups, she just took off and ran away to sea. So Grandma had to break all the china herself that day. And she wasn't used to it, the poor thing, so she got blisters all over her hands. She never saw Malin again. And Grandma said that was a shame, because she was such a marvelous maid."

Then Pippi left, and the ladies hurried on their way. But after they had gone a couple of hundred feet, they heard Pippi shouting in the distance at the top of her lungs:

"SHE NEVER SWEPT UNDER THE BEDS, THAT MALIN!"

Chapter Ten

Pippi Comes to the Rescue

One Sunday afternoon Pippi was wondering what to do. Tommy and Annika had been invited out to tea with their mother and father, so she couldn't expect a visit from them.

The day had been filled with pleasant activities. She woke up early and served Mr. Nilsson juice and rolls in bed. He looked so sweet as he sat there in his light blue nightshirt, holding the glass with both hands. Then she fed and groomed the horse, telling him a long story about her travels at sea. After that she went into the living room and painted a big picture on the wallpaper. The painting showed a fat woman in a red dress and black hat. In one hand she was holding a yellow flower and in the other a dead mouse. Pippi thought it was a very beautiful painting. It spruced up the whole room.

Then she sat down in front of
the cabinet and looked at all her
birds' eggs and seashells.
They reminded her of all
the wonderful places where

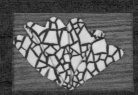

she and her pappa had collected
them . . . and the nice little shops
around the world where they had
bought all the fine things . . .

that were now in the
drawers of her cabinet.

After that she tried to teach Mr. Nilsson to dance the polka, but he didn't want to learn. For a moment she considered trying to teach the horse, but instead she crawled inside the firewood box and closed the lid. She pretended that she was a sardine in a sardine can, and it was so annoying that Tommy and Annika weren't there so that they could be sardines too.

But now it was starting to get dark. She pressed her little potato nose against the windowpane and looked out at the autumn twilight. Then she happened to think about the fact that she hadn't been out for a ride on her horse for a couple of days, and so that's what she decided to do. It would be a pleasant way to end a most agreeable Sunday.

She put on her big hat and went to find Mr. Nilsson, who was sitting in a corner playing with some marbles. Then she saddled the horse and lifted him down from the porch. And they all rode off, with Mr. Nilsson sitting on Pippi and Pippi sitting on the horse.

It was quite cold, with ice on the roads, and the horse made a great clattering noise as they raced along. Mr. Nilsson sat on Pippi's shoulder and tried to catch hold of a few tree branches as they rode past. But Pippi was riding so fast that he couldn't do it. Instead, tree branches kept slapping against his ears as he rushed by, and he had difficulty keeping his straw hat on his head.

Pippi rode through the little town, and everyone anxiously squeezed up against the walls of the buildings as she stormed past.

Of course the town had a marketplace. And on the market square stood the little town hall, which was painted yellow, and several beautiful old single-story buildings. A big monstrosity of a building stood there too. It was a newly built four-story structure that was called the Skyscraper, because it was taller than all the other buildings in town.

On this particular Sunday afternoon the little town seemed very quiet and peaceful.

Suddenly the quiet was shattered by loud shouting: "The Skyscraper is burning! Fire! Fire!"

People came running from all directions, their eyes wide. A fire engine drove through the streets with its siren going, and the children of the town, who usually thought it was so much fun to see the fire engine, were now crying in terror because they thought their own houses were going to catch fire too. In the market square a big crowd had gathered outside the Skyscraper, and the police were trying to keep everyone back so the fire engine could get through. Big flames were shooting out of the Skyscraper's windows, and smoke and sparks enveloped the firemen who bravely began to put out the fire.

The fire had started on the ground floor but spread quickly to the upper floors. Suddenly the people who had gathered in the square caught sight of something that made them all gasp with horror. At the top of the building was an attic room. A small child's hand had just opened the attic window, and there stood two little boys, shouting for help.

"We can't get out because someone has made a fire on the stairs," shouted the bigger of the two.

He was five years old, and his brother was a year younger. Their mother had gone out, and there they now stood, all alone. Many people in the square started to cry, and the fire chief looked worried. The fire engine did have a ladder, but it wouldn't reach nearly high enough. And it was impossible to go inside the building to get the boys. Despair descended on the people in the square when they realized that nothing could be done to rescue the children. And the poor boys stood up there, crying. It wouldn't take long before the fire reached the attic.

In the middle of the crowd gathered in the square sat Pippi on her horse. She looked with interest at the fire engine, thinking that maybe she would buy one for herself. She liked it because it was red and because it had made such a racket as it drove through the streets. Then she looked at the crackling fire, and she thought it was fun to see sparks falling around her.

Eventually she noticed the little boys up in the attic. To her surprise they didn't seem to think that the fire was particularly fun. She couldn't understand why. Finally she had to ask the people standing around her, "Why are those children screaming?"

At first she got only sobs in reply, but at last a portly gentleman told her, "Well, why do you think? Wouldn't you be screaming if you were up there and couldn't get down?"

"I never scream," said Pippi. "But if they really want to come down, why isn't anyone helping them?"

"Because it's impossible—that's why," said the portly gentleman.

Pippi pondered this for a moment.

"Can someone bring me a long rope?" she said.

"What good will that do?" said the portly gentleman. "The children are too young to climb down a rope. And besides, how would you get the rope up to them?"

"Oh, I learned a thing or two while I was at sea," said Pippi calmly. "What I need now is a rope."

No one thought it would do any good, but Pippi got her rope all the same.

A tall tree grew at one end of the Skyscraper. The crown of the tree was about the same height as the attic window, but between the tree and the window was a gap of almost three yards. And the tree trunk rose straight up, without any branches to use for climbing. Not even Pippi would be able to climb that tree.

The fire was blazing, the children in the attic were screaming, and all the people in the square were crying.

Pippi
got
down
from
her
horse
and
went
over
to
the
tree.

Then she took the rope and tied it to Mr. Nilsson's tail.

"Now you need to be Pippi's good little boy," she told him. And she put him up on the tree trunk and gave him a little shove. He knew perfectly well what he was supposed to do. And he obediently climbed up the tree trunk. For a little monkey it was no problem at all.

The people in the square held their breath as they watched Mr. Nilsson. Soon he reached the crown of the tree. There he sat on a branch and looked down at Pippi. She signaled to him to come back. And he did, but he climbed down on the other side of the tree branch. When Mr. Nilsson was back on the ground, the rope was looped over the branch and now hung down double with both ends touching the ground.

"You know what, Mr. Nilsson? You're so clever that you could be a professor any time you like," said Pippi as she untied the knot that held one end of the rope fastened to Mr. Nilsson's tail.

Close by stood a house that was being repaired. Pippi ran over and found a long plank. Then she put the plank under her arm, raced over to the tree, grabbed hold of the rope with her free hand, and then braced her feet against the tree trunk. With nimble speed she climbed up the trunk, and the people stopped crying out of sheer astonishment. When she reached the tree's crown she placed the plank across a thick branch and cautiously slid it over to the attic window. The plank stretched like a bridge between the tree and the window.

No one down in the square uttered a sound. They were speechless with suspense. Pippi climbed out onto the plank. She gave the two boys in the attic a friendly smile.

"You look so sad," she said. "Do you have a stomach ache?"

She ran across the plank and jumped in through the window.

"It's awfully hot in here," she said. "You're not going to have to heat the place any more today, I guarantee it. And I think four sticks of wood in the stove tomorrow should be plenty."

Then she picked up a boy in each arm and climbed back out onto the plank.

"Now you're finally going to have some fun," she said. "This is almost like walking a tightrope."

And when she reached the middle of the plank she lifted one leg in the air, exactly as she had done in the circus. Then a gasp went through the crowd down in the square. A second later, when Pippi dropped one of her shoes, several elderly women fainted. But Pippi safely reached the tree with the boys, and then all the people down in the square gave a cheer that thundered through the dark evening and drowned out the roar of the fire.

Pippi hauled up the rope and fastened one end tightly to a branch. After that she tied the other end around one of the boys and slowly and cautiously lowered him down to his overjoyed mother, who was waiting in the square below.

She instantly threw her arms around her son and hugged him with tears in her eyes. But Pippi shouted, "Hey, untie the rope! There's another boy up here, and he can't fly either."

So everyone helped untie the knot to set the first boy free. Pippi was certainly good at tying proper knots! That was something she had learned at sea. Then she hauled the rope back up, and it was the other boy's turn to be lowered down.

Now Pippi was alone up in the tree. She jumped onto the plank, and everyone looked up at her, wondering what she was planning to do next. Pippi danced back and forth on the narrow board. She raised and lowered her arms beautifully and began to sing in a hoarse voice. The people standing below in the square could barely hear the words:

A FiRE is burning,
it's burning so hot,
it's burning in circles so bright.
It's burning For YOU, it's burning For ME,
it's burning For those who dance in the night!

180

And as she sang, her dancing got wilder and wilder, and many of the people in the square shut their eyes in fright because they thought she was going to fall and be killed. Huge flames were shooting out of the attic window, and in the glow of the fire the crowd could see Pippi quite clearly. She raised her arms toward the evening sky, and as a shower of sparks fell over her, she shouted loudly, "What a fun fire this is! How fun, how fun!"

Then she leaped for the rope.

"Here I come!" she shouted, and then she lowered herself to the ground with the speed of greased lightning.

"Three cheers for Pippi Longstocking! Long may she live!" shouted the fire chief.

"Hurrah! Hurrah! Hurrah!" cried all the people. But one person gave four cheers instead of three. And that was Pippi.

Chapter

11

Pippi Celebrates Her Birthday

Do not bend.

One day Tommy and Annika found
a note in their mailbox.

TO TMMY AN ANIKA

it said on the envelope. And when they
opened it they found a card that said:

TMMY AN ANIKA SHUD COME TO
PIPPIS HOUSE FOR A BURTHDAY
PARTEE TOMORO AFTERNOON.
U CAN WARE WATEVER U LIKE.

That made Tommy and Annika so happy that they started jumping around and dancing. They had no problem understanding what the card said, even though the spelling was a little odd. Pippi had gone to a great deal of trouble to write it. Now it's true that she had said she didn't recognize the letter "i" that day when she went to school, but the fact was that she actually did know how to write—at least a little. When she was sailing the seven seas, one of the sailors on her father's ship would sometimes sit with her on the quarterdeck in the evening and try to teach her to write. Unfortunately, Pippi was not a very patient student.

In the middle of everything she might say, "No, Fridolf" (the sailor's name was Fridolf), "no, Fridolf, I just don't care about all this. I'm going to climb up to the crow's nest and see what the weather will be like tomorrow."

That's why it wasn't so strange that she had trouble writing. She spent a whole night working on that invitation. Then early in the morning, just as the stars were beginning to fade over the roof of Villa

Villekulla, she slipped over to Tommy and Annika's house to put the note in their mailbox.

As soon as Tommy and Annika got home from school they started dressing up for the party. Annika asked her mother to curl her hair, which she did. She also put a big pink silk ribbon in Annika's hair. Tommy combed his hair with water so that it would stay nice and flat. He certainly didn't want to have curly hair. Then Annika wanted to put on her very best dress, but her mother didn't think that was a good idea. Annika was never very clean or tidy when she came home from visiting Pippi. So Annika had to settle for her next-best dress. Tommy didn't care much about what he wore, as long as he looked more or less presentable.

They had bought a present for Pippi, of course. They took the money out of their own piggy banks, and on their way home from school they went into a toy shop on Storgatan and bought a very nice . . . Well, let's keep it a secret for a little while longer. The present was now wrapped in green paper and tied up with plenty of string. When Tommy and Annika were ready, Tommy picked up the package and they set off, as their mother anxiously warned them to be careful about their clothes. Annika also wanted to have a turn carrying the package, and they agreed that when it came time to give the present to Pippi, they would do it together.

It was now well into November, and twilight came early. As Tommy and Annika walked through the gate of Villa Villekulla, they were holding each other's hands tightly because it was quite dark in Pippi's garden. The old trees, which were just about to lose the last of their leaves, rustled so glumly. "Sounds like autumn," said Tommy. How much nicer it was to see lights in all the windows of Villa Villekulla and to know that they were going to a birthday party there.

Usually Tommy and Annika would race down the kitchen path, but today they went up to the front entrance. The horse wasn't on the porch. Tommy knocked politely on the door. From inside they could hear a muffled voice say:

On this dark night, who do I see
coming up the path to my house?
Is it a ghost, or could it be
only a poor little mouse?

"No, Pippi, it's us," cried Annika. "Open the door!"
Pippi opened the door.

"Oh, Pippi, why did you say that part about a ghost? I got so scared," said Annika, forgetting all about wishing Pippi a happy birthday.

Pippi laughed heartily and threw open the door to the kitchen. Ooh, how wonderful it was to come into all that light and warmth! The birthday party was going to be held in the kitchen, because that was the nicest room. There were only two other rooms on the ground floor. One was the living room, which had only one piece of furniture, and the other was Pippi's bedroom. But the kitchen was big and spacious, and Pippi had decorated it so nicely. She had put rugs on the floor, and on the table was a new tablecloth that Pippi had made herself. The flowers she had embroidered on it looked a bit strange, but Pippi claimed that those sorts of flowers grew in Farthest India. So everything was as it should be. The curtains were drawn, and a crackling fire blazed in the stove. Mr. Nilsson was sitting on top of the firewood box, banging two saucepan lids together, and over in the far corner stood the horse. Naturally, he was also invited to the party.

Now Tommy and Annika finally remembered to wish Pippi a happy birthday. Tommy bowed and Annika curtsied, and then they handed her the green package and said, "Many happy returns of the day." Pippi thanked them and then eagerly tore open the package. And inside was a music box! Pippi went wild with delight. She hugged Tommy and she hugged Annika. She hugged the music box and she hugged the wrapping paper. Then she wound up the music box, and with much plinking and plunking it played a tune that was probably supposed to be "The More We Get Together."

Pippi kept winding it up again and again, and she seemed to have forgotten about everything else. But suddenly something occurred to her.

"Oh dear, I have to give you your birthday presents too!" she said.

"But it's not our birthday," said Tommy and Annika.

Pippi looked at them in surprise. "No, but it's *my* birthday, isn't it? Surely I can give you birthday presents too, if I like? Or does it say in one of your schoolbooks that it's not allowed? Is there something about **pluttification** that says it shouldn't be done?"

"No, of course it can be done," said Tommy. "It's just not customary. But I, for one, would love to have a present."

"Me too," said Annika.

So Pippi ran into the living room to get two packages that were sitting on the cabinet. When Tommy opened his package, he found a little flute made of ivory. And in Annika's package there was a beautiful pin shaped like a butterfly.

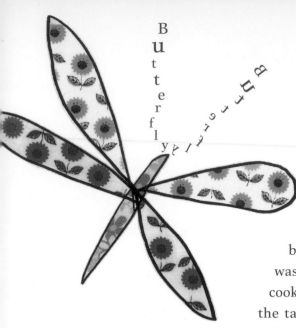

Butterfly

Butterfly

The butterfly's wings were set with red, blue, and green stones.

After they had all opened their birthday presents, it was time to eat. Piles of cookies and rolls covered the table. The cookies had a rather peculiar shape, but Pippi claimed that they had cookies just like that in China.

Pippi poured cocoa with whipped cream into their cups, and then they were all supposed to sit down.

But Tommy said, "Whenever Mamma and Pappa have dinner parties, all the gentlemen are given cards that tell them which lady they're supposed to escort to the table. I think we should do that too."

"Let's do it," said Pippi.

"Although it won't be easy for us, since I'm the only gentleman here," said Tommy doubtfully.

190

"Oh, nonsense," said Pippi. "Or maybe you think that Mr. Nilsson is a lady?"

"No, of course not, I forgot about Mr. Nilsson," said Tommy. And then he sat down on the firewood box to write the cards.

"'Mr. Settergren has the pleasure of escorting Miss Longstocking.' Mr. Settergren—that's me," he said, sounding quite pleased as he showed Pippi the card. Then he wrote the next card.

"Mr. Nilsson has the pleasure of escorting Miss Settergren."

"Yes, but the horse has to have a card too," said Pippi firmly. "Even though he won't be sitting at the table."

As Pippi dictated, Tommy wrote another card. It said: "The horse has the pleasure of staying in the corner, and there he'll get cookies and sugar."

Pippi held the card under the horse's nose and said, "Read this and tell me what you think."

Since the horse had no objections, Tommy offered Pippi his arm and escorted her to the table. Mr. Nilsson made no attempt to invite Annika, so she decided to carry him over to the table. But he refused to sit in a chair, so he sat on the table. And he didn't want any cocoa with whipped cream either. But when Pippi poured water into his cup, he grabbed it with both hands and drank.

Annika and Tommy and Pippi munched and crunched, and Annika said if these were the sort of cookies they had in China, then she was going to move to China when she grew up.

When Mr. Nilsson had emptied his cup, he turned it upside down and put it on his head. When Pippi saw this, she did the same thing, but since she hadn't finished drinking her cocoa, a little stream trickled down her forehead and ran down her nose. But Pippi just stuck out her tongue to stop it.

"Wouldn't want to waste a drop," she said.

Tommy and Annika first thoroughly licked their cups clean before putting them on their heads.

When everyone was content and full and the horse had been given what he was supposed to have, Pippi took a firm grip on all four corners of the tablecloth and picked it up, making the cups and cookie plates clatter together as if they were in a sack. She stuffed the whole bundle into the firewood box.

"I always like to clean up as soon as I've finished eating," she said.

And then it was time to play. Pippi suggested that they play a game called "Don't Step on the Floor." It was very simple. The only thing they had to do was to move around the whole kitchen without touching a foot to the floor. Pippi climbed all the way around in a flash. But even Tommy and Annika could do it. They started at the kitchen sink, and if they stretched their legs far enough they could reach the stove and then go from the stove to the firewood box, from the firewood box to the hat shelf and down onto the table, and from there across two chairs to the corner cupboard. It was six feet from the cupboard to the kitchen sink, but fortunately that's where the horse was standing. They could climb up his tail and then slide down his head, and if they jumped at just the right moment, they would land in the kitchen sink.

After they'd been doing this for a while, Annika's dress was no longer her next-best, but rather her next-next-next best, and Tommy was as covered with grime as a chimney sweep. They decided to think of something else to do.

"Let's go up to the attic and say hello to the ghosts," suggested Pippi.

Annika flinched.

"Are there g-g-ghosts in the attic?" she asked.

"Are there! Tons of them," said Pippi. "It's crawling with all kinds of spooks and ghosts up there. You practically trip over them. Shall we go up there?"

"Oh, Pippi," said Annika, giving her a reproachful look.

"Mamma told us that there's no such thing as spooks or ghosts," said Tommy staunchly.

"And she's right," said Pippi. "Except for here, because all of them live in my attic. And it doesn't do any good to ask them to leave. But they're not dangerous. They just pinch your arms hard enough to leave bruises, and then they howl. And they use their heads as bowling balls."

"They use their heads as b-b-bowling balls?" whispered Annika.

"That's exactly what they do," said Pippi. "Come on, let's go up and talk to them. I'm an excellent bowler."

Tommy didn't want to show that he was scared, and he actually wouldn't mind seeing a ghost. It would be something he could tell the other boys at school. Besides, he took comfort in the fact that the ghosts probably wouldn't dare go after Pippi. So he decided to go along. Poor Annika wanted nothing to do with the whole thing, but then it occurred to her that a tiny little ghost might come slinking downstairs as she sat all alone in the kitchen. And that did it! She'd rather be with Pippi and Tommy and a thousand ghosts than be all alone in the kitchen with the smallest ghost child!

Pippi went first. She opened the door to the attic stairs. It was pitch dark. Tommy kept a tight grip on Pippi. And Annika kept an even tighter grip on Tommy. Then they went up the stairs. There was a creaking and squeaking with every step they took. Tommy started to wonder whether it might have been better to stay behind. Annika didn't need to wonder—she was sure of it.

Eventually the stairs ended and they were standing in the attic. It was completely dark except for a little strip of moonlight on the floor. A sighing and whistling came from every nook and cranny as the wind blew through all the cracks.

"Hey, all you ghosts!" shouted Pippi.

But if there actually was a ghost, he wasn't answering.

"I should have known," said Pippi. "They've all gone to a board meeting of the Spooks and Ghosts Association."

Annika uttered a sigh of relief. She hoped that the meeting was going to last a very long time. But just then a horrible sound came from a corner of the attic.

Clay-oo-eet, they heard, and the next instant Tommy saw something come rushing toward him in the dark. He felt it flutter against his forehead, and then he saw something black disappear out through a little window that stood open.

He screamed to high heaven, "A ghost, a ghost!"

And Annika joined in.

"The poor thing is going to be late for the meeting," said Pippi. "If it was a ghost, that is—and not an owl!" After a moment she went on, "By the way, there's no such thing as ghosts. So the more I think about it, the more likely it seems that it was an owl. And if anyone claims that ghosts actually exist, I'll twist their nose."

"Yes, but you said that yourself," said Annika.

"Is that right? Did I really?" said Pippi. "Well, then I guess I'm going to have to twist my own nose."

And she took a firm grip on her nose and twisted it.

After that Tommy and Annika felt a bit calmer. They were even brave enough to venture over to the window and peek out at the garden. Big black clouds were moving across the sky, doing their best to hide the moon. And the trees were rustling.

Tommy and Annika turned around. But then—oh, how horrible!—they saw a white figure coming toward them.

"A ghost!" Tommy shrieked wildly.

Annika was so scared that she couldn't even

scream. The figure kept coming closer, and Tommy and Annika clung to each other and shut their eyes.

But then the ghost spoke.

"Look what I found! Pappa's nightshirt was in an old sea chest over there. If I take up the hem I could actually wear it."

Pippi came over to them with the nightshirt dragging around her feet.

"Oh, Pippi, I almost died of fright," said Annika.

"But nightshirts aren't dangerous," Pippi assured her. "They don't even bite—except maybe in self-defense."

Pippi now decided to look through the sea chest properly. She carried it over to the window and threw open the lid so that the faint moonlight would fall on the contents. There were a lot of old clothes, which she tossed out onto the attic floor. The chest also contained a telescope, a couple of old books, three pistols, a sword, and a bag of gold coins.

"**Tiddly-pom** and **piddly-dee**," said Pippi with delight.

"How exciting!" said Tommy.

Pippi gathered up everything in the nightshirt, and then they went back down to the kitchen. Annika was very happy to get out of the attic.

"Never let children handle guns," said Pippi as she picked up a pistol in each hand. "Or else an accident might easily happen," she said, firing both pistols at once. "What a loud bang that was!" she said, looking up at the ceiling. They could see two bullet holes.

"Who knows?" she said, sounding hopeful. "Maybe the bullets went straight through the ceiling and hit some of those ghosts in the leg. That should teach them to stop and think twice the next time they plan to scare any innocent little children. Because even if ghosts don't exist, that's no reason for them to scare people out of their wits. By the way, would you each like to have your own pistol?" she asked.

Tommy was thrilled, and Annika wanted one too, as long as it wasn't loaded.

"Now we can start a band of robbers if we want to," said Pippi, holding the telescope up to her eye. "With this I think I can almost see the fleas in South America," she went on. "It will also be a good thing to have if we're going to start a band of robbers."

Just then someone knocked on the door. It was Tommy and Annika's father, who had come to take his children home. He claimed it was long past their bedtime. Tommy and Annika hurried to say thank you and good-bye and gather up all their belongings—the flute and the butterfly pin and the pistols.

Pippi followed her guests out to the porch and watched them go down the garden path. They turned around and waved to Pippi. The light from inside the house fell all around her. There she stood with her red braids sticking straight out. She was wearing her pappa's nightshirt, which dragged around her feet. In one hand she held the pistol and in the other the sword. She used the sword to present arms.

When Tommy and Annika and their pappa reached the gate, they heard her shouting something after them. They stopped to listen. The wind was blowing so loudly in the trees that they had to strain to hear her. But they did hear her.

"I'm going to be a pirate when I grow up," Pippi yelled. "How about *you*?"

Astrid Lindgren. The year 2007 marks the 100th anniversary of Astrid Lindgren's birth. Lindgren was born and grew up on a farm called Nas, near the town of Vimmerby, Sweden. As a young woman she moved to Stockholm, where she held various jobs including reader and translator, married, and became the mother of a son and a daughter. She began to write stories about Pippi to entertain her daughter Karin, and the first Pippi Longstocking book was published in 1945. Many other books followed, and in 1958 Astrid Lindgren was awarded the Hans Christian Andersen Medal, the highest international award in children's books. Spirited, irreverent, and outspoken, Lindgren was beloved in Sweden, where she campaigned for an Animal Protection Act, and against high taxation. She died in 2002.

Pippi Longstocking was first published in the United States in 1950, and has been translated from the original Swedish into ninety-one languages. Feature films and television shows continue to be made about Pippi, who is truly a heroine for our time. Why do we love Pippi? Because, like Astrid Lindgren, she is fearless, independent, original, and lives exactly how she chooses.

Astrid Lindgren photograph by Jacob Forsell. Lauren Child photograph by her father.

Lauren Child was born in 1967 and grew up in Marlborough, England, the middle one of three sisters. Both parents are teachers, and they introduced her to Astrid Lindgren's books. Lauren says, "I discovered Pippi Longstocking when I was eight years old and found her completely inspiring. She caught my imagination, influenced my games, and has had a lasting impact on my work. I suppose the real key to Pippi is that she is an entirely free spirit: she is a girl who is both exciting and funny, refreshing to encounter even after all these years." Lauren has created some memorably feisty girl characters of her own, including Clarice Bean and Lola, of the Charlie and Lola stories. Lauren Child lives in London. Visit her at www.milkmonitor.com.

Tiina Nunnally is widely acknowledged as the preeminent English translator from Scandinavian languages. Her numerous awards include the PEN/Book of the Month Club Translation prize for the third volume of *Kristin Lavransdatter*. She grew up in Milwaukee in a Finnish-American family and received an MA in Scandinavian studies from the University of Wisconsin. She loved reading *Pippi Longstocking* as a child, and is thrilled to be the translator of this new edition. Tiina Nunnally lives in Albuqerque, New Mexico. Visit her at www.tiinanunnally.com.